Painting
Caitlyn

Painting Caitlyn
Text © 2006 Kimberly Joy Peters

Published by Lobster Press™
1620 Sherbrooke Street West, Suites C & D
Montréal, Québec   H3H 1C9
Tel. (514) 904-1100 • Fax (514) 904-1101 • www.lobsterpress.com

Publisher: Alison Fripp
Editors: Alison Fripp & Meghan Nolan
Editorial Assistant: Morgan Dambergs & Molly Armstrong
Graphic Design & Production: Tammy Desnoyers

We acknowledge the financial support of the Government of Canada
through the Book Publishing Industry Development Program (BPIDP)
for our publishing activities.

The Canada Council   Le Conseil des Arts
for the Arts   du Canada

We acknowledge the support of the Canada
Council for the Arts for our publishing program.

Library and Archives Canada Cataloguing in Publication

Peters, Kimberly Joy, 1969-

    Painting Caitlyn / Kimberly Joy Peters.

ISBN-13: 978-1-897073-40-7
ISBN-10: 1-897073-40-2

    I. Title.

PS8631.E823P34 2006   jC813'.6   C2006-900064-6

Printed and bound in Canada.

For Laurel

– Kimberly Joy Peters

Painting Caitlyn

written by
Kimberly Joy Peters

Lobster Press ™

Chapter 1

There are some things you can't admit to anybody: not to your parents, not to your friends, not even to yourself.

Maybe it's because saying it out loud, acknowledging it, makes it more real. And the more real it is, the more frightening it becomes.

That's how it was for me.

But eventually, the truth has to come out, and you have to take all the little bits and pieces of your life that didn't seem to matter by themselves, and pick them up again, and shake them around, and put them back together into one big picture. And then you have to look at it, and you have to be honest about what it really is.

And sometimes, you have to stand back a little to see that truth. My self-portrait is like that. I spent so much time working up close, examining, perfecting, critiquing the small details – the curve of my lips, the mole on my cheek, the curl of my hair – that I couldn't see what was really wrong, why it just didn't look right. Now I know.

In the end, it wasn't really about *me*: it was all about *him*.

I hadn't met Tyler yet when I found out that I was finally going to have a baby brother or sister.

I say "finally" not because I'd been waiting for one – I'd given up on that idea long ago – but because my mom had been trying for so long to get pregnant again, and it was a dream *she* wouldn't give up on.

With me, it was easy. Accidental, actually. She was twenty years old, in college, and she got pregnant with her boyfriend. They never got married or anything. My mom says he left because he was too young and immature to be a parent, and he gave her full custody, and that's why I never see him.

He ended up moving out to the West Coast right after I was born. I only met him once, when he was back here for a business trip and I was about four years old. But I was so little that I mostly just remember the restaurant where we met him, because it had a big goldfish pond with a waterfall right in the middle of the restaurant. I spent almost the whole time looking at the fish, so I don't really remember my dad. After lunch, we stopped at a pet store, and he got me a goldfish to take home. I named it "Goldie."

Goldie died pretty fast, and I cried for days, and I kept hoping my dad would come back and buy me a new fish. My mom kept cursing him for giving me a pet in the first place.

Anyway, that was the last time I saw my "real" dad. I used to ask my mom about him, but she'd always just tell me that he moved a lot, and she didn't know where he was. When I tried looking him up on the Internet one time, I got about a thousand hits for his name – everything from politicians to parolees – so I don't know how I'll ever track him down by myself.

But you can't miss somebody you don't really know, right?

Anyway, my mom married Mike, my stepfather, when I was seven, and they'd been trying to give me a little brother or sister ever since.

Even after they married, I still didn't call him "Dad."

Mike started going out with my mom when I was about four, and I mostly liked him, because he used to take me to the zoo and everything, but now I think he was just doing that to suck up to my mom, and make her think he was okay with having a kid around. I was excited when they got married, because I got to be a flower girl, and wear this lacy pink dress my mom picked out for me while I carried a basket of flowers down the aisle. I thought it was so cool that at the reception I asked my mom if she could have another wedding the next day.

My happiness quickly evaporated. When they left for the honeymoon, my mom said, "Kiss Daddy goodbye," and I realized they weren't taking me with them. I was so mad, I decided then and there that I was *never* going to call him anything except Mike. And I never did.

I think it hurt his feelings when I used his first name. Now that I'm older, I totally understand why they wouldn't have wanted a little kid like me tagging along with them on their honeymoon, but I'd called him Mike for so long that I couldn't really imagine calling him anything else.

It's weird, thinking about my mom having sex. First, she obviously did it with my real dad, probably sneaking around the way Tyler and I did, because she was still living at home. And then with Mike, she didn't actually say, "We had sex last night, and it was great," but she talked about how they were still "trying for a baby."

I didn't know why another baby was so important to her, but it was. I used to think maybe something was wrong with me – that I wasn't pretty enough, or smart enough, or maybe she'd wanted me to be a boy, but she said it wasn't that – it was just that she wanted more children, and she wanted to give Mike a child, and someday I'd understand.

So that kind of pissed me off too. That she wanted to give Mike a child. Didn't she already give him me? For all their talk over the past several years about how I'm his daughter, and he loves me like his own, why did he still need "a child of his own" with my mom? Like I'm not his, never will be, and his own would be so much better. Maybe he *thought* it would be better, but I doubted it. For one thing, Mike has really big ears, and so do his dad, and his brother, and all the other guys in his family. There was no way that he could have a kid and not pass on those ears. I figured I'd end up with a brother or sister who looked like Dumbo.

My mom and Mike tried a whole bunch of things to get pregnant. For the first couple of years, while my mom was still in her twenties, the doctors just kept telling them to "relax." Then, when nothing was happening, they went in for testing, and it turned out that my mom had some plugged tubes or something, so she had an operation to try to fix it. After that, she was really happy for a few months, waiting to heal and thinking it would work. But then another few months went by, and a few more, and she still didn't get pregnant. It got so bad that sometimes, if she was supposed to go to a party or something where she knew people would have babies, she'd make up some excuse not to go. She said it was too painful to see everyone else with their perfect little families.

As a last resort, they did *in vitro* – you know, test-tube babies. My mom took a whole bunch of drugs, and had needles every day, and then they took some of her eggs and some of Mike's – stuff – (I get so grossed out even thinking about it), and mixed it all around, and then put it back in my mom. And finally, it took. She was pregnant.

I couldn't sleep the night they told me. Long after I had gone to bed, I took out my sketchbook and tried to draw my new family. I started with what I already knew. I drew myself: skinny – almost on the scrawny side, according to some people – with shoulder length strawberry-blond hair, and round green eyes. A mole on my cheek. Not bad looking, but probably nothing special, either.

Then, a little apart from me, because it seemed like we weren't as close as we used to be, I added my mom: a slightly older, heavier version of me, with darker hair (which she stopped bleaching in case it was making her not get pregnant), and a deeper tan (from the tanning salon – but the spray on kind, not the one from a tanning bed, because she was afraid the light from a tanning bed was also making her not get pregnant).

Mike was next. He's super tall – way over six feet – with dark hair and eyes, a moustache, and, like I already said, huge ears.

I drew him in with his arm around my mom, because he's very protective of her. One time, when I was about nine, he grounded me for two weeks for marching around the house when my mom had a headache. To this day, I think the punishment was totally excessive. I mean, I didn't know she had a headache, and I was just a little kid – he could have just asked me to stop. I think my mom should have done something to help me get out of the grounding, but she just said, "He's your father, and you have to abide by what he says."

I tried to sketch a baby into the picture next. I put it between my mom and Mike, because it would be theirs, but I'd already put Mom and Mike so close together that I couldn't really make the baby fit. And I had no idea how to do its face. I just couldn't picture a baby in our family, and I've never been good at drawing things from my imagination.

Unfortunately, along with the news that my parents had finally conceived came the news that I had to get out of my bedroom. My room was the one closest to my parents', so it had to be the nursery. They were going to fix up the guest room in the basement for me – like I wasn't a member of the family anymore, just someone crashing here for a couple of years until college, so why not drop me down below, out of sight?

And I didn't even have any time to get used to the idea of moving. Even though the baby was still months away from being born, Mom and Mike wanted me to change rooms as soon as possible.

"Because we need to decorate it as a nursery," my mom explained when I protested. "And because I can't paint while I'm pregnant, Mike will have to paint the nursery himself – so it makes sense for you to do your room now, while you're off for the summer and have time to do your own painting. Besides," she added, knowing she didn't quite have me yet, "there's always a possibility that this baby could come early."

I knew very well that the baby could come early – I'd heard enough about baby-making to know that if you have trouble getting pregnant in the first place, you might have more trouble making it all the way through nine months without something going wrong. Plus, my mom wasn't exactly young anymore. Part of me was actually thinking she shouldn't be making such a public display of her pregnancy – telling everyone, making me move out of my room and everything – until it was more of a "done deal." Like it was bad luck to be counting on it already.

But I knew better than to challenge her or burst her bubble, so when she pointed it out, I just turned and left the room.

And I didn't talk about it with anyone – not even with my best friend, Ashley – for a long time.

Like I said, all of this happened just before I met Tyler. At the time, I knew that the new baby was going to be a huge change. But I had no idea how many other things in my life were about to shift.

Chapter 2

Tyler first noticed me at an amusement park, in the splash pool. Not so remarkable, really, when you think about how many kids hang out there every summer, except that I'd gone there with Ashley and her boyfriend, Brandon.

Ashley had been going out with Brandon for eight months, and I'd been feeling left out a lot because the two of them spent so much time together. Even when I tagged along with them, it felt awkward sometimes, because they'd end up kissing and giggling together, and it made me wonder if they'd really rather be out alone.

That day at the park, though, it was Brandon who introduced Tyler to me.

It was the end of July, right before our second year

of high school, and between the Ashley/Brandon lip lock and the stuff with my parents, it had been a crappy summer. Everything seemed to turn around for me, though, the day I met Tyler.

Blond hair, dimples, and dark blue eyes that made the sky look wimpy and pale. He looked pretty good in a bathing suit too, with his summertime tan. The hair on his legs and chest told me that he was older than the boys in my class, and it made him seem more mature.

But the best part was, even though I wasn't very experienced with guys, I knew right away that he liked me. He kept looking at me, even when he was talking to someone else, and he smiled a lot, and put his arms around my waist in the wave pool, supposedly to hold me up as the water came crashing through. Sometimes he didn't let go right after the waves, but kept holding onto my waist, strong and confident, with his big hands warm against my bare skin. It was almost like we were dancing to a slow song in a dark, crowded gym.

Afterwards, the four of us went for burgers. I found out that he was a year and a half older – sixteen already – and he went to another school, but he knew Brandon because they played baseball together all summer.

We all made polite small talk while we ate, then Brandon and Ashley started fooling around – holding hands, gazing into each other's eyes, nibbling on each other's ears, stuff like that – and the conversation was left up to Tyler and I.

"Do you do any sports?" he asked me.

"Not really," I confessed, hoping he wasn't just interested in athletes. "I'm pretty klutzy."

"Well you looked pretty good in that pool today – are you sure you're not a swimmer?"

"Hardly." I could feel myself blushing. That's the problem with red hair: it goes with fair skin, and you can't hide embarrassment when you have fair skin. The blushing always gives it away.

"So what *are* you good at?" he asked, with a little smile that made me wonder whether it was really just an innocent question.

"Caitlyn's a fabulous artist," Ashley broke in. I hadn't realized she'd been listening. "Isn't she, Brandon?"

"Yeah, pretty good, I guess," Brandon mumbled as he nuzzled his face into the side of Ashley's neck. She giggled and turned to kiss him back, signaling that she was done with the conversation.

"Really? You're an artist?" Tyler leaned in. "Do you draw, or paint, or what?"

"Drawing, painting – whatever. It's really just a hobby. I'm always trying to get better," I said. I was embarrassed that Ashley had even brought it up. As soon as someone says something like that, everyone wants to see my work, and then I feel as if they're judging me by it.

"I bet you're already pretty good. You have very dainty fingers. That probably means you have good control for delicate work – you know, like a surgeon." As he said this, he leaned over and took my hand in his so casually that we might have been going out forever, like Brandon and Ashley. I glanced over to see if they'd noticed, but they were still making out, oblivious to everything else. I was relieved that Tyler was there, so that, for once, I had someone else to talk to while they were distracted by each other.

"Seriously," I said. "Not *that* great."

"That's not what my buddy Brandon says." He nodded toward the other side of the table. "So maybe you'll have to just let me see for myself sometime. Can I call you, or send you an email, or something, to set it up?"

"Umm, yeah – that would be okay, I guess." I hoped I didn't sound as immature, and excited, and weird as I felt.

It turned out that nobody in the group had a pen or paper, so we ended up using Ashley's eyeliner to write everything out on a paper napkin. I wished I had something better to write on, because I was kind of afraid that he'd just smoosh it up in his pocket, or blow his nose on it, or something, and forget about me.

That night, when I got home, I tried to sketch his

face. I wanted to capture it and keep it with me, because I'd felt so happy sitting there with him, and I needed to hold onto that, in case he didn't call. I had trouble with his nose and his lips, but I got the eyes perfectly right. They were so beautiful in their blue-ness that I knew them by heart, and I felt as if he were watching me get ready for bed.

I didn't have to worry about him not calling – I checked my email before I went to sleep, and found that he'd already sent me four separate messages.

I.

MISS.

YOU.

SWEET DREAMS.

As if I could sleep after a day like that! It was completely new and different for me to have the attention of a guy like Tyler, but I was really excited about it all.

I think Ashley was even more eager than I was for Tyler and me to be together.

"It's perfect," she told me on the phone the next day. "Tyler and Brandon are friends, and we're friends, so now we can all hang out together. Maybe someday you and I will end up married to Brandon and Tyler, and we can have kids at the same time, and take them back to the water park ..." She rattled on and on.

One of the great things about Ashley is that she puts herself wholeheartedly into whatever she's doing. If she's writing an essay, it's guaranteed to get an "A." If she's baking a cake, it's not only delicious, but beautifully decorated too. Unfortunately, her enthusiasm means that she also has a habit of getting carried away with things, and that was actually part of the reason that I was so happy Tyler liked me. Ever since Ashley and Brandon had gotten together, I'd hardly seen her. She once told me that "your friends will always be there, but you have to work at keeping your boyfriend." Right or wrong, she was focusing on Brandon as much as possible, figuring I'd always be there, waiting around, ready to hang out with her when he was busy or out of town.

I'd never come right out and told her how annoying it actually was, being her second choice for company every weekend, having to listen to how perfect Brandon was, or why he was the most horrible person she knew (depending, of course, on her mood, and how their last date had gone). I missed her, but I knew I was probably just jealous because she had a boyfriend, and I was pretty much alone without her.

Tyler called right after I got off the phone with Ashley.

"Is it okay that I'm calling?"

"Perfect. Your timing couldn't have been better. Honestly."

"You didn't answer my emails, so I wasn't sure if I should even call ..."

"I didn't want to seem too desperate," I confessed.

"Desperate for what?" he teased.

"I don't know – what do you have to offer?"

"Well, I could have offered my heart, but I met this girl yesterday and she didn't email me back last night, and now my heart is crushed, so that's a 'no-go,'" he said. "What do *you* have to offer?"

"An apology for not getting right back to you, and for crushing your heart?"

"Apology accepted, but you're going to have to make it up to me."

"How?" I asked.

"I'll think of something ..."

We talked on the phone for two hours. When we hung up, he said, "Goodbye, beautiful."

Beautiful.

No guy had ever come right out before and told me that I was cute even – let alone beautiful. I hardly slept again that night because I kept thinking about it.

"Sexy" was the word Ashley used. "Tyler told Brandon he thinks you're sexy," she said later.

"Are you *serious*?" I asked. "Beautiful" was good, but "*sexy*" was unbelievable.

"Totally serious," she assured me.

"Why do you think he's interested in me?" I asked her.

"What do you mean '*why is he interested?*' Didn't you hear what I just said? He thinks you're *sexy!*"

"Yeah, but that's what I don't understand," I confessed. "He's almost two years older than me, he drives, and he's totally gorgeous. He could probably have any girl he wants, and there are *way* sexier girls out there. So why is he even interested in me?"

"I don't know! Just be happy, and don't mess this up, okay?"

I knew she was right and I should just "be happy," but I was really afraid that I *would* mess it up. I didn't have a lot of experience with guys. I'd had guys like me before, but it never seemed to be the ones I was most interested in. I was really hoping I could make things work out with Tyler.

Chapter 3

Tyler and I emailed and talked every day from then on. By the time we had our first "official" date the next weekend, I felt as if I'd known him forever. I knew that he had an older brother in college; I knew that he played almost every sport imaginable; I knew that he liked pepperoni on his pizza, and ketchup on his macaroni and cheese (but not on his French fries); and if he could only have music or television for the rest of his life, he'd choose television.

When the weekend finally arrived, we went on a double date with Brandon and Ashley. Ashley was sleeping over at my place, and the guys were going to pick us up there. I expected my parents to have a fit over the fact that Tyler was older and had his own car; but at that point they were so preoccupied with the success of their test-tube baby, and scheduling and sorting out what doctors appointments they had, that they really weren't paying a lot of attention to what I was doing. Plus, they knew I was with Ashley and Brandon, so that helped too.

We were going to a party out at the lake. Brandon and Ashley made out in the backseat while Tyler drove. I sat next to him, totally embarrassed to be back with him in person, and suddenly not knowing what to say. He looked at me and smiled a lot, and he whistled along with the radio. He seemed really confident and relaxed, and I liked that about him.

When we arrived, the party was in full swing. The stars were shining, a huge bonfire roared on the beach, and there were couples making out all over the place.

"You want to go for a walk?" he asked. I nodded, wanting to say yes, but afraid that I'd say something stupid if I opened my mouth. I *really* wanted to make a good impression.

He took my hand in his, and we walked beside the water's edge.

Away from the fire, it was cold. On Ashley's recommendation, I'd worn a good pair of shorts and a cropped T-shirt that showed off my figure, but now I shivered and regretted my choice in clothes.

"You must be freezing," he said, and he turned to face me, putting his hands on my waist.

"A little ..." I started to explain, but before I could finish, he'd pulled me in close, and murmured, "Well you'd better watch out, because I don't want you getting sick ..." And that's when he kissed me.

Up until that moment, I'd never really been kissed. I mean, I'd had stupid, little-kid kisses before at parties when we played spin-the-bottle and some poor guy got stuck with me, but that was it. Usually the guy would just roll his eyes and give me a peck on the cheek, or a quick brush of the lips if the host demanded it, but I'd never kissed anybody for *real* before.

It was better than any kiss I'd ever imagined.

I hoped I was doing it right.

I remembered all the teen magazine articles I'd read about kissing that said to just let it happen, breathe normally, part your lips a little, tilt your head – but how exactly do you breathe normally while you're thinking about parting your lips, tilting your head, and whether or not you have fresh breath?

Plus, all the other guys I'd kissed had still been years away from any real facial hair, so the rough-textured scratchiness of his face surprised me. I felt his tongue brushing mine, lightly at first, and then stronger, as his hands crept up my back to my bra; and the whole time, all I could think was, "I am finally kissing a guy, and he is totally gorgeous." And I wasn't cold anymore. I couldn't tell whether it was the warmth of his hands on my back, or having his body pressed against mine, or whether I was just overheating from the thrill of kissing him, but I felt warm all over. We stayed on the beach kissing for several minutes, and even though part of me wanted to rush back and tell Ashley all about it, another part of me never wanted it to end.

I told Ashley all about the kissing later that night, back at my place. She couldn't believe I'd actually let him touch my bra, and I couldn't believe the way she reacted.

"Oh my God!" she shrieked. "You are a *total slut!* I didn't let Brandon anywhere *near* my bra until we'd been going out for a *month!*" she giggled in joking disbelief.

I knew she was teasing, but I was kind of sorry I'd told her.

I wasn't sorry that it had *happened*, just that I'd told Ashley about it.

I mean, it wasn't like he'd actually *undone* my bra, or touched my breasts underneath it, or anything. It was more like his hands just sort of ended up there on my back because of the short top I was wearing. And really, I didn't see how it was any different from the first day at the water park when he saw me in my bathing suit, but somehow Ashley seemed to think I'd done something wrong.

We were crashing on the floor of my bedroom, whispering because I didn't want my parents to wake up, and I totally didn't want them to overhear; but Ashley just kept shrieking with every detail – and then she started picking it all apart.

Sometimes she acts as if she knows everything – and the truth is, I used to think she did. She gets good grades in school, which is one of the reasons we started hanging out together years ago – because back in public school, it wasn't cool to be smart, and we were both "A" students. In sixth grade, when another kid started teasing me about being a teacher's pet, Ashley told him it was better to be a "pet" like me than a "pest" like him.

I wished I'd thought of standing up for myself the way she stood up for me. We've been friends ever since.

It's different in high school, where we're all competing for the best spots at the best colleges and universities. Now it's okay to be bright, and some people even admire you for it. Ashley's one of the smartest people I know.

Not only is she smart, she's got pretty, long black

hair that lies smooth and flat for her every day, no matter what the weather, and I don't think she's ever had a pimple. My mom once described her as the kind of girl you'd love to hate, but she's just so nice you can't help loving her.

Anyway, she's good at standing up for herself and for other people, but she has a tendency to go to extremes. Maybe it's because she's used to having all the right answers in school, but when she decides that she's right and everyone else is wrong, there's no convincing her otherwise.

That night, after the beach party, she seemed so genuinely shocked by my first date with Tyler that a little part of me started to wonder if I really had let things move too quickly.

But even though Ashley made me question whether I'd let things go too far too soon, I also wondered whether a little part of her was just jealous because Tyler was so much more confident than Brandon, and it hadn't taken him as long to make a move.

I hoped Tyler didn't think I was too "easy."

Sometimes I wondered whether people had thought my mother was "easy" when she got pregnant with me. She'd been going out with my dad for a long time before it happened, but still, she was young, and she wasn't married, and people might have judged her negatively because of it.

I spent most of the rest of the night worrying about my reputation, and being mad at Ashley.

Until very recently, before we had boyfriends, Ashley and I did almost everything together, and she slept over all the time. We did all the regular girl stuff – tried on makeup, made up dance routines, sang karaoke into the mirror. And talked about guys. We talked about them endlessly – who was hot, who was nice, what qualities we wanted in the men we were going to marry – assuming, of course, that we decided to get married. Her mom had already been married three times, so she wasn't sure it was worth the bother, but I think that's why she worked so hard at making Brandon number one.

At first, when she started going out with Brandon, I didn't mind hearing all about it – it was kind of a natural progression from "*I wonder how he kisses*" to "*you'll never guess what he does when he kisses*," and I was totally happy for her. It got old really fast, though, because I never had anything to add to the conversation, and now that I did, I felt like she was being overly critical. She'd giggled and shrieked when she'd said I was a slut, but still, she *had* said it, and when she'd stopped laughing, she looked very serious again, as if she were trying to decide whether or not to say something else. So even though I knew she was probably just not used to me finally having something to contribute, I found myself straining to identify her tone of voice, and wondering how my best friend really felt about the new guy in my life.

Chapter 4

Tyler called me the next afternoon.

Wanting to find out how he felt about things, I tried to sound casual when I raised the subject of the bra-touching incident. "You know, I really like you," I said.

"I really like *you*," he teased back, and my heart felt like it was flipping around inside me again – the same way it had when he'd kissed me.

"Well, that's what I wanted to talk to you about," I explained. "I mean, I'm not usually that, um ... open with guys I've just met, and Ashley thought you might have gotten the wrong idea about me last night ... so I just wanted you to know that I'm not usually like that ..." I babbled.

He was quiet at first, and I was afraid I'd scared him

off with all the "I like you" stuff, but then he spoke up.

"You told Ashley what happened between us?"

"Well, just the main stuff," I explained. "You know, that we kissed. That you put your hand on my back. That kind of thing. She *is* my best friend."

"Some friend!" he snorted. "She's got you all stressed out, thinking you did something wrong last night, when *she* wasn't there, and all you did was kiss a guy who's nuts about you, and it's none of her stupid business anyway. How fair does that sound?"

I had to admit that he was right. She really didn't seem to understand how romantic it all was, and she *had* made it all sound kind of dirty.

"Maybe you shouldn't worry so much about what Ashley thinks," he continued. "In fact, I don't think we should discuss our relationship with Brandon and Ashley at all."

"Not at all?" I remembered all the times that Ashley had come moaning to me over Brandon. I had sort of been looking forward to doing the same with her, asking for her advice, giggling over the cute things Tyler was bound to do. And now he was saying that I shouldn't bother with her.

"Well, obviously we're going to double date with them sometimes," he softened, "but what goes on between us is really nobody else's business, don't you think?"

And when I *did* take the time to think about it, it all made perfect sense. After months of listening to Ashley going on and on about every move Brandon made, I finally had my own boyfriend to talk about, but all she wanted to do was criticize. Tyler was right – we should keep it private and special, just between the two of us. I was happy that he felt the same way. We were totally compatible. We had a *relationship*. We made plans to get together again that night.

Other than the beach walk, it was going to be the first time we'd been alone together. He came to pick me up in a different car than the night before, because his dad owned a car dealership.

"We always have different cars around at our place," he explained. "So I can pretty much just drive what I want."

Tyler was taking me to his house to watch a movie. He lived in a really nice part of town, which I'd already suspected because of the school he attended. His neighborhood was filled with big, newer houses with two- or three-car garages, and a lot of swimming pools. His house was a long redbrick ranch style, with an interlocking-cobblestone driveway.

The property itself was large, with lush green grass like you'd find on a Florida golf course, but that was as far as the landscaping went. There wasn't a tree or a shrub or a flower in sight, and the house struck me right away as out of place and incomplete, like a woman in a fancy dress at a formal party who has forgotten her makeup and jewelry.

Our home suits my mother perfectly. It's clean and pretty on the outside, but underneath, it's older than it looks, with a couple of bits that are kind of wobbly and not as secure as you'd think.

Looking at Tyler's house, I wondered what his parents might be like.

I didn't get to meet them that night, as it turned out. We had the place all to ourselves.

"No dog?" I asked, as we entered the silent house.

"No dog. Why – were you expecting one?"

"More like *hoping* for one, I guess. I've always loved dogs and I've always wanted a puppy, but Mom and Mike always say we're too busy, and it wouldn't be fair to have a dog around. Ashley and I used to walk her dog together every day after school until she started seeing Brandon. Now he usually goes with her."

"*I* like walking with you," Tyler said with a wink, "and you can rub my belly any time you want, but I'm sorry I don't have a dog for you to play with. We had one once, but we had to give it away because my mom's allergic. Do you want a glass of water or anything?"

He was headed for the kitchen, but I was still

thinking about dogs.

"You had to give it away? That must have been horrible!"

Tyler shrugged. "I guess."

"I can't imagine having to give away a dog. I had a goldfish once, and I was really sad when it died ..." I told him the story of Goldie and my dad while we ate cookies in his kitchen.

Tyler put his arm around me as we toured through the rest of the house. Like the outside, the inside felt as if it were missing something. The furniture was new and modern, with a lot of leather and hardly any fabric. The colors were cool whites and neutrals. Everything was so simple and uncluttered that it almost seemed as if nobody had ever lived there. It struck me as being very cold and lonely. There were a few pieces of sculpture, but there was hardly any art on the walls.

Tyler's room was completely different from the rest of the house. He had posters all over the walls – posters of girls. There were girls in bathing suits, girls in shorts, even some girls who weren't dressed at all. I couldn't believe his mother would let him have stuff like that in his room – there was no way my parents would *ever* let me have naked guys on my walls, and, anyway, I would have been too embarrassed to even try it.

"Oh my gosh!" I blurted out. "You have so many

naked women in here!"

"Mmm ... but not *enough* naked women," he joked, reaching for the buttons on my blouse.

I swatted him away in what I hoped was a playful manner. "Not so fast," I said. "First you have to tell me about all these other girls."

"What about them?" he asked, flopping down on his waterbed.

"Where'd they come from?"

"Calendars, magazines, the Internet mostly," he said.

"I thought guys were supposed to hide stuff like that in the backs of their closets," I said, only half-joking.

"Yeah, well, I like looking at them, so they're not much use in the closet."

"Don't your parents mind?" I asked.

"My mom doesn't like them," he said, "but I don't care if she does or not. It's my room, and I do what I want with it. And anyway, I think my dad kind of likes them, so he sticks up for me. Sometimes it helps to have parents who disagree. Anyway, I'm the baby of the family, so my older brother kind of paved the way for me. It's probably harder for you, being an only child," he said.

When he mentioned me being an only child, I began to open up to him, and I finally told him about the thing that had been privately gnawing away at me for days: the fact that I was getting a new brother or sister. I told him everything – how I had to change rooms, and go to the guest room like someone who didn't even live there anymore; how I was beginning to feel like I was nothing but a mistake my mom had made, and *this* was the baby she *really* wanted, with her husband, after such a long time of trying; and how she'd probably love it more than she loved me, because she loved Mike, and I don't think she was ever in love with my father. It was the first time I'd said it out loud to anyone, and until then, it might as well have been a dream.

As I talked, I began to cry. He listened, told me it would be okay, and held me while I sobbed. He was so gentle and understanding that he made me feel safe and cared for, like no matter what happened at home, I had someone who thought I was special. When my tears stopped, he leaned over and kissed me.

We ended up making out instead of watching a movie that night as we'd planned. Kissing him made shivers run down my back. I didn't let him go under my shirt though, because we were in a bedroom and everything, and I kept thinking about what Ashley had said.

Chapter 5

Shortly after Tyler and I started going out, my parents decided that we should have dinner together as a family once a week. They wanted to establish some new traditions, they said. I thought it was ridiculous, since we hadn't done it before the baby, but, as with everything else, I wasn't allowed a veto.

At first, they didn't even want me to invite Tyler – they said it was just supposed to be the three of us, and that it was a time for them to catch up with me and the things going on in my life, so that they could still be involved. I told them Tyler *was* what was going on in my life, and if they wanted me there, he should be there too. That argument worked, and they agreed that it would be a good idea to meet "the young man I'd been seeing" (my mother's words).

We went to a restaurant. Tyler was pulling into the parking lot as we arrived, and I could tell right away that Mike wasn't very happy about him having a car.

"How long have you had your license?" Mike asked, after I'd made the introductions.

"Just a couple of months – since I turned sixteen," Tyler replied.

"So you're still a fairly inexperienced driver?" Mike shot back.

There was no way Tyler could get out of that one – he couldn't lie, because he'd already admitted it had only been a few months, but if he agreed, Mike would win.

"I'm certainly not as experienced as many older drivers, Sir, but I do take the responsibility seriously. I would never jeopardize your daughter's safety, if that's your concern."

Mike still wasn't pleased, but I thought it was a pretty good answer, considering he'd put Tyler on the spot like that.

The questions continued after we'd gone inside the restaurant.

"I understand you're also quite an athlete – how do you find time for schoolwork with such a busy schedule?" my mom asked. "Surely football must take up a lot of your time, and with a girlfriend on top of that – I know you two spend a great deal of time on the telephone – how can you balance all of your activities and still keep up with your schoolwork?"

"Tyler was on the honor roll last year," I told them. "I'm sure he can handle it."

The rest of the night was pretty much the same: them asking questions as if Tyler were on a job interview, and Tyler fending off the attacks with all the right answers. They couldn't come up with any real objections to him, though I felt like they'd really tried.

The best part of it all was that the whole time Tyler was answering questions with a perfectly straight face, he was holding my hand under the table, and squeezing it now and then, just to remind me that we were together. It didn't matter what my parents' verdict was.

In the end, they gave their stamp of approval, and told me I seemed to have made a great choice.

A flicker of trouble ignited my insecurities the day I started to paint my new room.

We'd been together about two weeks by then, and Tyler had offered to take me to the store to pick up the paint. I had chosen a pale mauve color, but he thought I should get blue.

"I really don't think you'll be happy with that purple color," he said.

"Why not? I love it," I told him.

"Don't you think it's a bit – I don't know – girlie?"

"Yeah, maybe, but in case you hadn't noticed, I *am* a girl – or do I need to remind you of that ...?" I stood on the tips of my toes to reach his lips and kissed him lightly.

"I'm just saying I don't really feel comfortable in a room with that kind of color. So if you see me spending any amount of time with you in there, you might want to reconsider and get something a little more tame," he said, holding out a pale blue paint chip.

I thought about his own stark white house. I could understand how growing up without any color at all might make you overly sensitive to other people's color choices – but I just couldn't see myself in a pale blue room.

"The mauve is the same color I already have ..." I explained.

"I know," he said. "So can't you change the color, now that you're changing rooms?"

"Not really – I just redecorated last year, and I spent a long time choosing the duvet cover, and the drapes, and everything to match. I'm really happy with it," I protested.

"Isn't there any other color you could use with the duvet?"

I was starting to get really frustrated – not just about

the paint color, but about the room change, the baby, and everything. It seemed like I didn't have control over anything anymore. It was bad enough that I had to move to the basement, but the idea of having to live with a color I didn't love made tears start in the corners of my eyes. I knew that if I opened my mouth to speak, I'd start to cry for real, so I just shook my head "no." There were no other colors that would work.

Tyler could tell I was upset, and he relented. He wrapped his arms around me from behind and kissed the side of my neck. "Hey – don't get sad. If you have to get the purple, get the purple. I'm just saying that if we're going to be a couple now, you should run stuff by me before you make any decisions so we can both be comfortable with the outcome. You want me to be comfortable, right?"

"Yes."

"Okay, so let's get the purple, and just consult each other from now on, okay?"

We got the purple paint, and Ashley and Brandon came over to help us put it on the walls. I didn't tell them why I was changing rooms – I just let them think it was because I wanted to be down in the basement. We ordered pizza for dinner, put on a movie, and then Ashley and I made out with our boyfriends on the couch. Even though everything was changing, it turned out to be a great day.

My mom and Mike were happy that Tyler had helped me paint my room, and that having him around was cheering me up. I wasn't so focused on the baby anymore, because I had my own life and my own special person to think about.

We spent a lot of time together during August – just hanging out, watching TV, and being together. Somehow, everything seemed more special when I was with Tyler.

One night we'd ordered fried chicken, and just as we were about to take it to the park for a picnic, a thunderstorm roared in. We drove down by the water instead, and ate the food in his car, watching the rain stream down over the windshield as the lightning sprang out of the sky.

After the rain stopped, the clouds blew off, and the most amazing sunset appeared, with a double rainbow right over our heads.

"I feel like I'm in the middle of a *Disney* movie!" I said.

"... and you're the princess?"

"... and you're my handsome prince."

"Does that mean I get to kiss you?" he asked.

"It means you *have* to kiss me!" I whispered, leaning toward him.

"Do I have to save you from any monsters first?"

"Just the test-tube mutant sibling."

"Do you really think it's going to be that bad?" he asked.

"I don't know," I confessed. "I just think it's a creepy, weird way to have a kid, and it totally makes me feel like I'm going to end up being Cinderella, having to baby-sit and clean its filthy diapers and wipe its snotty nose, or my wicked stepfather Mike will be all over my case."

"He's not really wicked, is he?" Tyler asked, looking concerned.

"No," I sighed. "He's just really protective of my mom, and once he has a baby with her, he'll probably be the same way with it. I'm going to be all alone."

"You'll never be all alone – you've got me now," he said, wrapping his arm around me. "And your prince will always fight for his princess."

I snuggled in, and we watched the last of the sunset. I'd never felt so safe.

By the time summer came to an end, things were serious. I was still worried about going too far too fast, but Tyler told me not to stress about it.

"You like what we're doing, right?" he asked me one

night when I mentioned my concern.

"Yeah – well, mostly."

"What do you mean "mostly"?" he asked, sounding hurt.

"I mean, I do. I love kissing you, and having you touch me, and everything ... it's just that everything's moving really fast, and I don't want to do anything that we're going to regret ..." I said.

"I could never regret anything that had to do with you," he said, kissing me on the forehead.

"I know ..." I said, trying to explain. "I just never used to understand how it felt to really, really like someone, and now I really, really like you, and sometimes I can't think about anything else ..."

"I really, really like you too, Caitlyn," he said. "So *don't* think about anything else."

I *did* keep thinking about him. And us. And how if we really, really liked each other, maybe it was okay to show it.

From then on, we moved very quickly past "over the bra" and into "everything but ..."

Chapter 6

*A*s the school year began, I was trying to figure out how Tyler and I would be able to see each other as much as we'd become used to during the summer.

I would have loved to be like Ashley, sitting on my handsome boyfriend's lap in the cafeteria after lunch, sneaking a kiss at our lockers between classes, or even just holding hands in the hallway. I was so proud to be Tyler's girlfriend that I wanted the whole world to know it. But he went to another school across town, so I resigned myself to another year of trailing along behind Ashley and Brandon.

Ashley and I didn't have any classes together that year, but my good friend Conner was in my art class. We'd had classes together before, but we'd really gotten to know each other a few years earlier, when we were both in the art club, and Conner and I ended up working together on a mural in the school cafeteria. Until then, I hadn't realized that guys and girls could be "just friends." We spent a lot of hours painting the wall together, and by the end of it, we were pretty close.

In addition to being a fun guy to talk to, Conner is an amazing artist, and I admire him deeply because he is my total opposite. He's not quiet and introspective like me. He has this flamboyant personality, which means he'll come in with blond hair one day and red the next. One day, when I'd brought in some old jewelry to decorate masks we'd made, he bartered with me, trading me an earring out of his left lobe for a bracelet because he wanted it for himself. A few kids at school think Conner is gay, but I know he's not – not that it would matter if he was – he's just too smart for most girls.

One of the great things about art class is that we don't have to be quiet like in other subjects – we can play music if we want to, and we get to talk. I couldn't wait to talk to Conner about Tyler, and maybe get a guy's perspective on things like "how far is too far."

"So someone's finally won your heart? What's he like?" Conner asked with genuine interest.

"He's gorgeous, and sensitive—" I started to tell him, but he cut me off.

"Nope. This is art class. You have to describe him *artistically*," he teased. "If he were a color, what color would he be?"

It was a game we'd invented the year before, as a way to secretly gossip about teachers. A boring teacher, for example, would be "battleship gray," while an inspiring one would be "sunset saffron." Conner liked to joke that if he couldn't make it as a professional artist, at least he could get a job naming lipsticks for a cosmetics company.

"Princely Purple," I said, playing along. "Deep, rich, passionate, jewel-toned purple."

"Hmm ... and what medium would he be?"

"Acrylic paint," I said.

"Why? Is he artificial?" Conner asked.

"No, acrylics are bright, but tough."

"What's tough about him?" Conner asked, with a confused expression.

"He plays football. He has to take the tackles, move fast ..."

"He moves fast, does he?" Conner said, with a devilish grin.

I felt myself blush. "No, I mean, he *runs* fast."

"Okay, so he's definitely not a still life ..." Conner continued. We played the game for almost the whole class. As always, I was amazed by how much imagination he could put into a few simple questions.

It's his imagination that really makes Conner's art stand out. He can pull fabulous images out of his dreams and turn them into truly original works of art.

I'm good at doing lifelike pictures when I've got a model or something real right in front of me – even a photograph works well – but I'm useless when it comes to sketching from memory or, worse, from make-believe.

Some days, sitting next to Conner, I felt like I was more of a photocopier than an artist, because I could paint realistically, but I didn't have any creative spark. I couldn't even add a tiny baby to a family portrait because the baby didn't exist yet, and I didn't have enough imagination to pretend it did.

I saw the difference between my abilities and Conner's last year when one of our assignments in art class was to sketch something in a bottle or jar that wouldn't normally be found there. I spent hours doing a detailed copy of the city skyline inside a wide-mouthed mason jar. My perspective was perfect. My highlights and shading gave the illusion of depth. But the subject matter, for all of my efforts, was boring.

Conner drew a human figure, crouched naked and ashamed, trapped like a bug caught and preserved by a pre-schooler. He said it kind of represented how he felt about high school – like everyone was looking at him, judging him, and there was no way out. He'd used his heart and imagination for the assignment, when all I'd used were my eyes. That's why I sometimes feel like an imposter when I get to class.

My art teacher, Mrs. Van der Straeten, disagrees. She says that art is a gift regardless of where we find our inspiration, and that technique is just as important as subject. I kept getting "A's" from her on my projects, but deep down, I didn't think I really deserved them.

That year, she wanted us to do independent study projects in addition to our regular class work. One part of the project had to be an artist study – a biography; and the other part had to be a big studio piece – some artwork that takes almost the whole semester to plan and execute. For the studio piece, I chose to do a self-portrait in oil. It wasn't very creative, but I figured, since I'm good at copying, it would be easier than trying to come up with something new or abstract.

When I told Tyler about it after school, he wasn't so sure.

"You're doing a picture of yourself?"

"Yup. It's going to be huge, like something in a gallery or a big old mansion," I told him. "I have to do the whole thing myself, start to finish, including stretching and priming the canvas – and it's independent study, so it's fifty percent of my grade, but I have to do a lot of it on my own time."

"You're not going to be naked in the picture or anything, are you?" he asked.

I couldn't stop myself from giggling over that one – it was just so funny to picture myself sitting in art class naked, staring in the mirror, trying to paint!

"Of course I am," I lied. "All great portraits are nude – think of Renoir, Degas – plus, I know how much you like to see naked women on the wall ..."

"No way in hell am I going to let you do a nude painting of yourself," he fumed. "That's the sleaziest thing I ever heard!"

The anger in his voice was surprising. As much as he was getting to know my *body*, he obviously didn't know my *personality* well enough yet to be able to tell when I was goofing around. It was kind of reassuring to know that he worried about me, and about my reputation, but I didn't like the edge in his voice.

"*Relax!*" I told him. "I'm just kidding. I can't believe you'd take me so seriously!"

"What do mean, you can't believe I'd take you so seriously? Don't you *want* me to take you, and our relationship, and the things you say *seriously*? Don't you think a guy should be able to have a *serious* conversation with his girlfriend? I was *seriously* worried about your reputation, because I thought you were about to do something really stupid, and now you're trying to turn it around and tell me *I* screwed up? Do you want to rethink your position *at all*?" he asked.

That's when I knew he wasn't like other guys – he was so worried about me and my reputation; and he wanted to have serious conversations with me, not just stupid little "what did you do at school" discussions. It was so sweet that it made me feel really bad about joking around the way I had.

I guess maybe he didn't know me well enough to know that there was no way I would have *ever* posed nude for a painting, but until that moment, *I* didn't know *him* well enough to understand that he didn't like that kind of teasing.

Chapter 7

On the third day of school, a Thursday, Tyler surprised me. I was coming out of art class, right before lunch, and there he was, standing in the hallway waiting for me with a big bouquet of roses.

I'd been talking to Conner about meeting during lunch to work on our art projects, but I was so happy to see Tyler that I dropped my books in the middle of what Conner was saying and ran over to kiss my boyfriend.

"What are you doing here?" I asked.

"Taking you out for lunch, if your other boyfriend doesn't mind," he said, looking at Conner.

"Tyler, Conner. Conner, Tyler," I made the quick introduction. "And no, he doesn't mind, because he knows *you're* my boyfriend."

"Mmm," Tyler mumbled, after Conner had left. "I'm not sure he *does* know I'm your boyfriend. I think you should steer clear of that guy – he seems awfully interested in you."

"Conner? No – he was just interested in the art project we were talking about. He's doing a portrait too. Anyway, we've been friends for years – I hardly think he's interested in me!" I laughed.

We went to a fast food place near the school, and Tyler could barely keep his hands to himself. I was kind of self-conscious about it, though, because there were a lot of other kids there who I recognized from school.

I didn't really mind that he had his hand on my thigh the whole time we were eating, but when he tried to slip it up under my shirt, I got embarrassed and pushed him away very gently.

"Tyler! There are other people here."

"So?"

"*So* I don't want to be rude!" I said.

"So you want to let them put their hands up here too?" he teased, reaching for another feel.

"No, I just don't think this is the right time or place," I said.

"You don't really care about me, do you?" he asked, pulling his hand away.

"Yes I do! I didn't say I didn't care about you ..."

"Then can't you show that you care? That's what *I'm* doing – showing I care! But if you have a problem with affection, maybe I'll take these flowers – and the necklace I was about to give you for our six-week anniversary – and go give them to someone who doesn't mind when I try to show how much I love her!" As he spoke, he pulled a small jewelry box out of his pocket.

"You love me?" I almost wondered if I'd heard him wrong.

"Yes, Caitlyn, I do. I love the way you smile, and the way you say my name, and I love being with you. And that's what today was supposed to be about – celebrating six weeks together with a girl who made me fall in love with her ... but I'm getting really scared that you don't feel the same way, because you're not acting like someone who loves me back."

I felt so stupid then. He'd cut class to surprise me for our anniversary, bought me flowers and lunch, and then he'd pulled out this perfect little gold necklace with a heart-shaped pendant and one little diamond right in the middle; *plu*s he'd said he loved me. And what had I done for our anniversary? Nothing. Nothing except make plans to go to the art room at lunch with another guy, and then push away the guy I really liked when he tried to show how much he cared about me.

Before I could even process what he'd said, he

started to walk away, and I began to cry.

"I'm so sorry!" I blurted out. "I'm just not good at this stuff yet, because you're the first boyfriend I ever had who really cares!"

He was coming back by now, and he took my hand. "Didn't you hear what I just said? It's more than caring, Caitlyn. I *love* you," he said. "But you really have to make up your mind about how *you* feel about *me*, because I'm getting a lot of mixed signals."

"I *know* how I feel about you," I told him. "I – I love you too. And I really want to find a way to show it."

"Do you mean that?" he asked.

I wasn't positive that I *did* mean it. I didn't totally know what love was, but I knew that I liked being with him, and that I'd felt kind of lost when he started to walk away; I knew that he made my heart race, and my palms sweat, and my body think about doing all kinds of things I'd never imagined I'd want to do; and I knew that when someone said "I love you," they expected you to say it back.

"Because if you do mean it," he said, "then let's get out of here right now and go to my house – my mom won't be home from work for hours."

"But I have two more classes this afternoon ..." I started to explain, before I realized that this was my chance to make it up to him.

He put the necklace on me. "I have to work tonight, Caitlyn," he said. "So if we don't go now, we won't be able to see each other again."

When he saw me hesitating, trying to figure out what I should do, he offered me a solution.

"I'll call the school for you and pretend I'm your father," he said. "Then you won't get in trouble for skipping off."

"I really want to," I said, still unsure about whether the third day of school was a good time to skip class. Tyler seemed to read my mind.

"Look, we want to celebrate our anniversary, right? And most of your teachers are probably still doing review stuff anyway – I know mine are. So let's go," he said, as he put his hand on my back and directed me out to his car.

We ended up having a great afternoon. We made out, watched TV, and made ice cream sundaes, which we ate on the back deck in the early-autumn sunshine. My new necklace sparkled in the light, and I had never felt happier.

The next day, we had a pop quiz in math based on the work they'd done during the afternoon while I was away. I tried to explain to the teacher that I'd gone home sick, so I couldn't do the quiz, but I don't think he really believed me.

Conner was annoyed because I hadn't shown up at lunch to work on our independent art projects the way we'd planned.

"You totally blew me off," he accused, when I saw him the next day.

"No, I actually didn't feel well, and I went home after lunch." It wasn't really any of his business, but I figured I might as well stick with the lie I'd told the teachers.

"Of course. Your boyfriend shows up with flowers, takes you to lunch, and you get a mysterious illness right afterwards. Happens all the time."

"I'm sorry, okay?"

"Whatever."

"Why does it matter so much, anyway?" I asked. "It's independent study – that means you do it *independently*. You didn't need me to get started."

"It's just polite to let someone know if you're not going to show up," he said.

"I told you, I didn't *know* I wasn't going to show up," I explained. "We went for lunch, I wasn't feeling good after, I went home."

"Caitlyn, I don't care what you did yesterday –

whether you were feeling sick, or whatever, but I do think you should know that I heard some kids talking about you yesterday afternoon."

"You did?"

"Yeah. Some of it was okay – they said you had a hot new boyfriend and he was all over you at the restaurant – but some of it wasn't so good."

"What do you mean, 'wasn't so good?'" I asked.

"Just be careful, okay?"

"I don't need to be careful – Tyler told me he loves me. He would never do anything to hurt me." I felt myself blushing as I said it.

"The fact that he says he loves you," said Conner, "is *exactly* why you have to be careful."

I was being cautious with what I told Ashley about Tyler and me, but I was surprised by her reaction when I told her about our "anniversary celebration."

"Look at the necklace Tyler got me," I said.

"Oh my gosh – it's beautiful! What was the occasion?"

"Our six-week anniversary."

"Six weeks?"

"Yup."

"Six weeks isn't even a real anniversary – it's not like "six months" or "one year" or anything. Why is he giving you such a fancy gift for an imaginary anniversary?" She looked confused.

"Actually, it's more of an '*I love you*' gift. He said he loves me – can you believe it?"

"Seriously?"

"Mmm hmmm." I twirled the necklace around between my fingers and smiled.

"Wow. That was quick."

"What's that supposed to mean?"

"Nothing. It's great. It's just really fast, that's all. Do you love him too?"

"Yes – I mean, I think so. I like him more than any other guy I've ever met. And I think about him all the time ..." My voice trailed off as I tried to mentally calculate how many times a day he crossed my mind.

"That's not love, that's infatuation," Ashley said.

"How would you know?"

"I looked it up last spring, on the Internet. To see if I loved Brandon. There are tests you can take."

"You don't need to take a test to see if you love someone. You're just supposed to know."

"Maybe, but you can feel healthy and still drop dead from a bad heart, so don't you think you could feel like you're in love but really just have a major crush on someone? That's what my mom says happened with her second husband – the crush thing, not the heart attack."

"Your mom's situation and my situation are two completely different things!"

"I'm just saying that it seems really soon for you guys to know if you love each other or not."

"Do you think your mother loved you when you were a baby?"

"Yes."

"Well how much time did that take? Did she have to wait for six months or a year to make *sure* she loved you?"

"No, parents just love their babies."

"No kidding," I said, thinking about my mom and Mike.

Ashley shrugged. "Maybe you're right. Maybe you do just *know*. I'm sorry I questioned you. Your necklace is really pretty, and if you're happy, I'm happy for you. Really."

Her words were supportive, but she still looked doubtful and a little bit concerned. I wondered whether she might be jealous because I'd received such a nice gift, or whether there was more to it than that.

Chapter 8

a few days after Tyler gave me the necklace, I finally worked up the nerve to show him some pieces of my art.

Usually it's hard for me to share my art portfolio. Maybe it's because it's something I feel like I'm good at, but it still never feels like I'm as good as I want to be. In any case, as our relationship developed, I found myself wanting to show Tyler more of my work, because I wanted to share everything about myself with him, and my art is personal.

"This is amazing!" he said, looking at the sketch I'd done of him the first night we met. "You did this from memory?"

"Uh huh."

"It looks almost like a black and white photograph,"

he said.

I tried to explain to him that I didn't think what I did was as good as what Conner does, but he wouldn't listen.

"So do you ever do anything with your art?" he asked.

"Like what?"

"I don't know – sell it?"

"I couldn't sell it – everything I do means something to me. I hate to even give it away."

"You should put it on display. Like in a gallery or something," he said.

"No gallery wants a pencil sketch by a fourteen-year-old girl," I told him.

"Almost fifteen," he corrected.

"Almost fifteen."

"Can I have this?" he asked, pulling out a pastel landscape I'd done in the spring.

"I just told you, I hate to give my stuff away ..."

"Just for a little bit. Let me borrow it. Don't you trust me?"

"I guess ..."

It was just over a week later that he picked me up outside school, grinning as if he'd just won the lottery.

"What are you up to?" I asked, as I slid into the seat beside him. "I can tell something's going on."

"We're going to the fair," he said.

"The fall fair?"

"Yup."

"Now? I thought we were going to go tomorrow night, with Ashley and Brandon."

"I want to show you something."

He wouldn't say anything else about it the whole way there – even after we'd parked, and paid admission, he wouldn't tell me where he was leading me. We snaked our way through the greasy smells of fried foods, and the harsh sounds of the rides, past the late afternoon crowds, and toward the exhibition buildings.

He led me inside to the displays – the part of the fair where people enter their pickles, and jam, and the biggest sunflower they can grow. We were standing amidst the "handicrafts" – pillows, and afghans, and other stuff like that. I didn't understand what hand-sewn quilts had to do with me until I turned around and saw the art displays.

There, in the middle of the room, was my pastel landscape – the one I'd "loaned" him a week earlier. He'd had it framed, and entered it in one of the fine art categories. It hung there proudly with two ribbons on it.

"You won first prize in your division – Landscape,

any medium – and first prize overall for Fine Arts entries: a $100 gift certificate for art supplies."

"$100?" I was stunned.

"Plus $25 for the division prize."

"For one of my stupid little landscapes?" I was scrutinizing the other entries, looking for reasons why my art should have been selected over so many others.

"Your artwork is not stupid, Caitlyn. It's beautiful, like you, and you need to have more confidence in your talent. That's why I entered it."

He kissed me, and the thing I felt most confident about right at that moment was his love for me.

Later that night, when I told my parents about the win, Mike said, "I wonder if this one will be an artist too?" as he pointed at my mom's belly. More and more, it seemed as if everything was about the baby – even the fact that I'd actually won something.

"Doubtful," Mom said, looking down with a pout. "She didn't get it from me."

"Well, artist or not, I can't wait to meet our new little addition!" Mike said, nuzzling his whole face into my mom's stomach, as if he were trying to peek through her belly button and see what the new baby looked like.

The win at the fair made me realize that since Tyler
and I had been spending so much time together during
the summer, I hadn't been sketching or painting as much
as I wanted to. I didn't mind at first, because it was so
exciting to be with him, but now that we were back in
school I could tell I was a little rusty.

The next day, Tyler came over to my house with a
video, which by now was really just an excuse for us to be
alone in the basement, and I pulled out my sketchbook to
do some doodling.

"What are you doing?" he asked.

"Just sketching."

"Why?"

"Because that prize really motivated me, and I'm
feeling kind of inspired now. Mrs. Van der Straeten says
there are lots of other competitions I could enter, and I
should start building my portfolio now in case I want to
take art at college after high school."

'"No – I mean why *right now*, when I'm here?"

"Why not?" I was puzzled, because he'd seemed so
supportive before.

"Because I thought we were going to spend some
time together ..."

"We are ... I'm still right here."

"But you're distracted."

"How is this any more distracting than the TV?"

"Well, it's not really the distraction so much as we can't hold hands or anything while you're doing that, and if that's what you'd really rather be doing right now, maybe I should just go," he said, as he stood up.

"Please don't," I said. "You're right, though - I am too distracted for the movie. How about I show you some more of my work instead? You can help me pick something to submit for the yearbook."

"Okay, but it'll cost you," he teased, puckering his lips for a kiss.

I kissed him, then led him into my room, where I pulled out a bunch of drawings from the year before.

"Who's this guy?" he asked, looking at a series of sketches that all featured the same subject.

"Ahhh – David," I said.

"David who?"

"David is a guy I had a crush on last year," I explained.

"These are drawings of some guy you went out with before me?"

"No, no," I corrected him. "I never said we went out. I said I had a crush on him."

"What's the difference?"

"The difference is, I drew him from yearbook pictures for almost three months, until I knew every facial expression he had. But he didn't even know I was alive, and still wouldn't if I walked right up to him today."

"Do you still have a thing for this guy?"

"*You're* the only one I have a thing for," I reassured him, planting a kiss on his gorgeous forehead.

"Then why do you still have these drawings?"

"What?"

"Why do you still have all these drawings of this guy you used to like if you only like me now, and this crush, or whatever, is over like you say it is?"

"Because they're part of my portfolio. I told you – I hate to get rid of stuff, so I keep all my sketches and doodles," I explained.

"Well I don't like it. You don't need to keep these."

"Why not?"

"Because you've got me now. You don't need David. And I don't really want you looking at pictures of him, getting all hot over another guy."

"What about all the naked girls and stuff in your room?" I asked.

"That's totally different," he said. "They're all strangers – models and actresses I'm never going to meet in real life. They're absolutely no threat to you. That guy in your drawings is a real person who you know, and I don't want the pictures around to remind you of how cute you think he is."

"I need a bathroom break," I told him. I didn't have

to go very badly, but he was acting stupid, and I wanted to have some space before I said something I'd regret later.

When I came back in, he was ripping up the sketches. And not just into a couple of pieces, either – he was tearing them over and over again into little tiny bits no bigger than my fingernail. In less than five minutes he'd managed to turn hours of work into confetti.

I lunged at him, trying to save my artwork and shove him away.

"What are you doing?" I screamed, tears pouring from my eyes. "Get away from them! Get away!"

"I'm just eliminating the competition," he said.

"*Leave them alone!*"

"If you love me, you shouldn't care about these drawings!" he roared, ripping another sketch apart.

"I *don't* love you – I *hate* you!" I screamed back at him.

His hand came out of nowhere and slapped me hard on the face, knocking me backwards onto the floor. I hadn't even seen it coming.

Chapter 9

Seeing me injured on the floor made him instantly apologetic.

"Oh God – I'm so sorry, I'm so sorry." He kept saying it over and over again. "I didn't mean to – it was an accident. I just felt so hurt when you said you didn't love me," he murmured, cradling me in his arms.

"Get out."

"Caitlyn – I'm so sorry. I can't tell you how sorry I am."

"Just go away," I said. I couldn't even look at him.

"Please – give me another chance, just one more chance, I love you so much ..." he begged. I could see the tears in the corners of his eyes.

I heard my mom coming down the stairs, and then

she knocked on the door.

"Caitlyn? Is everything okay?" she asked, popping her head in and quickly scanning the room. Her eyes rested on the shredded remains of my sketches.

I could have told her right then. I could have said: "Everything is definitely not okay. The person I thought I might be in love with has destroyed some of my artwork because he's jealous of a guy who doesn't even know I exist, and he just smacked me across the face."

But to tell her that, I would have had to believe it. And I didn't believe it. It didn't make sense that someone I trusted could hurt me on purpose and destroy my work. Something about the tears in Tyler's eyes and the way he was looking at me even made me wonder whether some of it had been my fault: whether I should have kept the drawings to myself, whether I should have reacted so strongly when he tore them up. He just looked so very, very sorry, and confused, and desperate that I couldn't believe he'd done any of it intentionally.

I still wanted to figure it out for myself, so I bent over quickly, with my back to the door, and began picking up the paper scraps off the floor.

"It's okay," I lied, hoping my voice didn't give me away. "I was just telling Tyler about this argument I saw at school. I guess I got a bit carried away during the reenactment." I glanced back over my shoulder, careful to swing my hair over the cheek that had been hit.

My mom frowned and said, "You certainly had me convinced! Maybe you should give up art and go into theater!"

"Maybe."

"I'm sorry if we disturbed you," Tyler added. He was smiling now, and his face had completely changed – there wasn't a shred of fear, or regret, or anger visible in his expression.

"Okay, then. I'll leave you two alone. But do me a favor and keep the door *open*, okay? I know what it's like to be young and in love," she said, as she turned to go back up the stairs.

My head hurt. And my cheek had a red splotch on it. I started to cry softly as soon as my mom was gone.

"Just because I didn't say anything to her doesn't mean I forgive you!" I hissed.

"I wouldn't blame you if you never wanted to talk to me again," he said. "But please, please, just know that I never meant to hurt you. It was an accident. I swear." He apologized over and over again.

I believed him when he said that the slap had been an accident, because it seemed like the only answer that made any sense, and he'd apologized; but I was still furious at him for destroying my work. That hadn't been an accident.

I told him to leave, and then I lay down on my bed and fell asleep.

Tyler showed up at two a.m. that morning. I don't know whether I woke up because I heard him tapping at my window, or whether I was already sort of awake and it just made me realize I wasn't dreaming.

I went upstairs to tell him to go away, but he was standing there with a teddy bear, and a giant sign that said, "I'm sorry."

I wouldn't take it, at first. I wasn't even going to open the door. I mean, it's not like a teddy bear could make up for what he'd done. I opened the heavy door to send him away, but then he started to beg through the screen.

"Please open up? Just let me talk to you. I am *so* sorry ..."

"Sorry's not going to replace my work, or completely make up for what happened," I whispered. "And if my mom and Mike hear you, it's not going to save your butt, either!"

"No – it won't – but you have to know that staying mad at me isn't going to fix anything ... is staying mad worth losing what we have? I know you don't want to throw our whole relationship away. I could see it in your eyes when your mom came downstairs. It's too late for me to go back and change things – and believe me, if I could, I would. I don't know why I did it – I just got so crazy jealous thinking about you wanting to be with some other guy – I couldn't stand it. You are so beautiful, and we are so perfect together – if you weren't the girl of my dreams it never would have happened. So even though I can't save the pictures, I have to try to save *us*, because that's what it was all about: me not wanting to lose you. And if you won't talk to me now, I'll stand out here until you go to school in the morning. Or the next day. Or whenever. You have to leave the house sometime, and I'm not giving up."

Even through the screen door, I could tell he was crying. Seeing him so upset got to me, and before I knew it, I was crying too. I went out and sat on the porch with him.

"How do I know it's not going to happen again?" I asked him.

"Because I'm so sorry. Because I never meant it to happen in the first place. Give me another chance. *Please.*"

"I don't know ..."

"I swear – I will be so good to you – everyone will be jealous because you have the best boyfriend ever. Please. Take me back. I promise I won't ever treat you that way again."

"I already told you I don't like Conner, or David, or anyone else – why isn't that enough for you?"

"Because you mean so much to me – I think about you all the time, and I just love you so much, I'm so sorry. I went crazy thinking about you and another guy."

"I haven't been interested in any other guy since I met you," I told him.

"Then prove it. Forgive me. Take me back. It will never happen again," he said.

So I did.

Chapter 10

*A*fter the night he "accidentally" hit me, Tyler went right back to being the sweet, considerate guy I'd first met. It was just as if nothing had happened.

Later that month, I turned fifteen, and Tyler was the best thing about my birthday.

The day started off looking like it was going to be great: my skin was clear, my hair looked awesome, and my mom made pancakes for breakfast even though it was a school day. I tried to tell her I wasn't a baby anymore, and she didn't need to make me the same birthday breakfast as always, but I was secretly glad she had. The rule in our house is that I don't get my present until after dinner, so I knew that would have to wait.

When I got to school, Ashley was waiting by my

locker. She'd decorated it for my birthday with wrapping paper, balloons, and streamers – a "best friends" tradition at our school.

"Happy Birthday!" she said, as I approached.

"Thanks!"

"But I have to tell you something before you get to your locker," she added.

"Brandon is going to jump out of it naked?" I teased.

"No ..."

"Good – 'cuz if anyone is going to jump out naked, I want it to be Tyler!"

"You've seen him *naked*?" she squealed, so loudly that a couple of other kids in the hall looked up.

"No!" I lied. "I was just kidding – you know, like when a lady is supposed to jump out of a cake at a bachelor party or whatever? Anyway, what did you have to tell me?"

"I'm really sorry, but someone messed with your locker. I decorated it last night, and when I came in this morning it was like that ..."

She stepped away from the locker, and I saw that, although it was beautifully decorated and even had "Happy Birthday" written on it in gold paint, someone had stretched a condom up over the lock.

It was gross.

I didn't want to touch it.

I felt like crying.

And I wondered where it had come from.

"That is so *disgusting*!"

"I know," Ashley sympathized. "I was trying to figure out how to get it off without touching it."

"Do you think it's been used?"

"I don't know – I mean – it looks kind of wet and slimy, but don't they come that way anyway?"

"You're the one with the long-term boyfriend ..." I told her.

"Yeah, well, we aren't like that – you know we aren't doing anything that needs a condom – and anyway, the bell's going to ring in five minutes and you need to get into your locker!"

Just then, Brandon arrived.

"Someone put a condom on Caitlyn's lock," Ashley told him.

"I can think of a better place to put it ..." he said.

"Dream on," Ashley said, as she rolled her eyes, and pretended to punch him in the arm. "Just help us out, will you?"

"What do you want me to do?"

"You're a guy – can't you take it off or something?"

"This isn't exactly how I've always pictured you asking me to remove a rubber ..." he said, "... so what's in it for me?"

"I won't tell your mother that you failed your geography test last week," Ashley said.

"Touché!"

And with one giant swoop, he pulled the condom off the lock, and tossed it into the trashcan.

"Was it ... umm ... used?" I asked, still wondering who would have done something like this.

"Ah ha! Now I *know* Tyler's not getting any, since his girlfriend's not up to speed on how to tell if a condom is fresh or previously enjoyed."

"You're not getting any, either, Mr. Smarty Pants," Ashley told him. "So shut up."

"Thanks for helping me out," I told him.

"No problem."

"Yeah, you *were* kind of heroic ..." Ashley said, as she grabbed a quick kiss.

The bell rang then, and we all ended up being late for homeroom.

Second period came, and I discovered that, in all the confusion, I'd brought the wrong books, and I lost marks for not being prepared. Even though I tried to explain to the teacher that it was my birthday, and it really wasn't my fault, she said it was no excuse.

Things got better just before lunch. As the bell rang at the start of the period, someone delivered flowers to the class. They were for me, from Tyler. The card was simple: *Looking forward to seeing you tonight, Birthday Girl! Love always, Ty.* Mrs. Van der Straeten was so impressed that she let me turn one of the old juice cans we usually use for rinsing paint brushes into a vase, and then she changed the whole lesson around to an examination of still life drawings so we could sketch the flowers in pastel.

Conner handed me an envelope at the end of class. Inside were a birthday card and a tiny paintbrush for doing very detailed work.

"Thanks," I said.

"No problem. Happy birthday," he told me, and then he winked, and walked away.

When I got home from school, I was surprised to see my mom's car already in the driveway.

"Mom?" I called as I went in the door.

"Up here!" Her voice was coming from her bedroom. I thought maybe she was doing some last-minute gift wrapping or something for me, but when I got up to her room I found her lying in bed, wearing her pajamas.

"Hi, sweetie. How was school?" she asked.

"It was okay," I said. "Why are you in bed?"

"I'm feeling pretty gross – looks like the morning sickness has moved on to all-the-time sickness. And I had some cramping. My doctor wants me to stay in bed for a couple days."

"But we're supposed to go out for dinner tonight!"

"I know, sweetie, but I can't go now, and Mike's going to have to take care of me, so you know what? Tyler called earlier and said *he'd* like to take you out, and I suspect you'd rather be with him than with your old mother, so I told him you'd be ready at five."

"Thanks. I'm happy to go with him, but I really wanted to go with you. I'm sorry you're feeling so sick."

"*I'm* sorry to bail on you like this."

"I know."

"Your gift is in my closet. Do you want to open it now, since we aren't going to dinner?"

"Okay."

I was hoping for a new easel and some oil paints of my own. That, or the puppy I ask for every year and never get. I knew *this* wouldn't be the year for a puppy either, with the baby coming and everything, but I'd still asked for one, just in case.

"I hope you won't be too disappointed ..." my mom said as I started unwrapping the package, which was way too small to be an easel.

It was an art book.

"I know it's not what you wanted, sweetie, but we spent so much money on the fertility treatments, and with the baby coming, we just can't afford a lot right now."

"No ... Mom ... it's beautiful, really."

"Do you like it? Mrs. Van der Straeten recommended it. It has short biographies of famous artists, and photographs of their work ..."

"I love it. I'll use it for my independent study project. Thanks." I kissed her on the cheek. "And tell Mike thanks too."

"I will. You'd better get going if you're going to be ready for five."

"Right." I stood up to go.

"... And Caitlyn? He said to dress warmly."

"Warmly?"

"Yes. And we've extended your curfew, now that you're fifteen."

"Thanks."

I went downstairs to my room and checked my email while I was getting ready. Tyler had sent me a personalized song from one of those Internet sites where you pick phrases to fill in, and then a song plays with all your choices. The first part was just regular birthday stuff, like, "Happy Birthday Caitlyn, Happy Birthday Dear, a very happy birthday, and a wonderful year." After that, he had put in some dirtier parts – like, "Wish

I was the candle on your cake, so you could lick the icing off me."

It was so hilarious, I laughed out loud – and my mom heard me from her bedroom.

"What's so funny?" she called down. I'd forgotten that the heating vent in my room went right upstairs to hers.

"Just a birthday email song from Tyler," I yelled back.

"Oh yeah? Turn up the volume so I can hear it."

"It won't go that loud," I lied.

"Well does it have the words with it? Print them out and bring them up so I can read them."

"My printer's out of ink," I lied again. "Anyway, I was just laughing because he said he wanted to buy me pink and purple polka-dotted penguins. You know, to match my purple room."

"You'll have to play it for me later, when I can get out of bed," she said.

I hoped she'd forget. There was no way I could let her hear – or see – the song. Especially now that she trusted me with a later curfew.

Tyler picked me up in one of his dad's sports cars, and took me out to the beach where we'd had our first kiss.

He set out a blanket, and built a small fire, and pulled a picnic out of the car. He'd thought of everything

– flowers, candles – even a small birthday cake.

"Let's go for a walk," he said, when we were done eating.

"Don't you think it's time for a new line?" I teased.

"Come on!"

It didn't matter that I'd dressed warmly. The winds were howling, and the waves were crashing on the shore, but I was so happy to be there with the guy I loved that I felt warm inside and out. Nothing could have ruined the moment.

"Look!" he said, pointing beneath a piece of driftwood. "It's a bottle with a message in it!"

I looked under the driftwood and, sure enough, there was a bottle with a piece of paper in it.

"What does it say?" he asked in mock surprise.

I pulled the top off and wriggled the paper out.

"Caitlyn's Magical Treasure Hunt," I read. "And it's a map!"

"*Caitlyn's* Magical Treasure Hunt? And on your birthday? Wow – what are the odds?" he joked.

I followed the clues on the map. Some of them were directions on where to go, like "turn left at the lifeguard stand," and some of them were instructions on things I had to do, like "kiss your boyfriend on the lips, so he can tell you which way to go from here."

The final directions were: "*Look up and look down,*

there's love all around. I give you the moon, and the stars, and all the gold on the beach."

"The moon, and the stars, and all the gold on the beach?"

"Yup. First, the moon," he said. Then he turned away from me, bent over, and pulled his pants down. A moon.

"Very funny, loser!" I swatted his bare bottom with the treasure map.

"You don't like it?" he asked, straightening up.

"You know I think you're cute all over ..." I said.

"... but?"

"... but nothing is how I expected it to be today," I confessed.

"Come here." He took me in his arms. "Look up – this is the part where I give you the stars. See right over there? That little tiny one just over Orion's shoulder?"

"Mmm hmm ..."

"That's yours."

"Mine?"

"Yours. I bought it for you through the International Star Registry, and now it's named after you. Forever."

"Seriously?"

"Seriously." He pulled a star map out of his pocket, with my own star circled in red, and certificate authenticating that a star had been named in my honor.

"That is the coolest thing ever!" I said as I hugged him. "I love you so much!" I felt like I could cry, it was so sweet and considerate.

"Don't you want the rest of your present?"

"The rest of it?"

"All the gold on the beach, remember?"

He took my hand and led me back to the edge of the beach, into a wooded area. Reaching under a bush, he pulled out a little goldfish bowl with a tiny goldfish inside.

"I know it's not a puppy – your mom said 'no way' when I asked – but I figured if your parents are getting someone small to love, you deserve the same. I thought maybe you could call him 'Goldie the Second,'" he explained.

I couldn't even talk, I was so happy with this tiny, perfect little fish, and my thoughtful, generous boyfriend.

Later that night, I tried to tell Ashley about it. I described everything: the picnic, the beach, all the sweet things Tyler had said to me, and how it was one of my best nights ever.

"That's awesome," she said. "Brandon and I went to the movies – we had a good time too."

She didn't get it. Brandon and Ashley *always* had a good time. My night was special because *everything* was perfect. And for the first time since school had started, Tyler didn't get upset about anything.

Chapter 11

*A*fter my birthday, I tried even harder to keep things good between us.

I made sure that I was available to see him when he wasn't working or playing football, and I tried to show him how important he was to me by focusing only on him, not homework or drawing, when we did get to see each other.

Mostly, it seemed to be working. The one area where I was having trouble keeping him happy was our physical relationship, because he wanted to take it "all the way" and I hadn't quite made up my mind yet.

"What's the matter?" he asked with exasperation one night when I'd gently pushed his hand away.

"Nothing ..." I tried to kiss him, to show him that

I cared.

"Then what's stopping you? I love you so much, Caitlyn ... I want to show you how much," he murmured, slipping his hand back over my breast.

"I kind of want to, I just don't know if I'm ready," I whispered, searching his expression to make sure he knew I wasn't rejecting him completely.

He got very serious as he stroked my hair and said, "What can I do so you'll feel ready?"

"I don't know ..." I hesitated, trying to put into words all the things I was feeling. "It's just a really big step."

"But it's a step I think we're ready for," he said. "We love each other, and," he added, "we can be really careful so you don't get pregnant or anything."

Even though he was trying to reassure me, it didn't help. I knew from health class that there was always a small chance of an accident even if we were careful, but it wasn't just that I was concerned about getting pregnant like my mom did with me. I was thinking about other stuff, like how I'd always thought my first time should be special, with me looking beautiful and him looking handsome; and how we should have all the time we'd want together, and not have to rush in the back of a car or on the couch before our parents got home.

There were other worries too, crouching in the back

of my mind. They were worries that I couldn't identify or articulate, but they were holding me back, making me want to wait.

"I love you, and I love being with you, but I need more time," I told him.

"Okay," he sighed. "But I hope time will change your mind ..."

Time was something I needed in other areas of my life too. I didn't have as much time with Tyler as I wanted, and I didn't have enough time to get all my homework done.

Later that night, after a family dinner at my house with Tyler, I was trying to figure out how to get my canvas home from school the next day so that I'd be able to put in some time on my painting over the weekend. There was really no way for me to bring it on the bus, and my mom couldn't pick me up because she had a doctor's appointment to go to ... again. Mike was going with her, of course. I was frustrated.

"I really wanted to work on it this Saturday," I said. "Can't you change your appointment?"

"I'm sorry, but I have to schedule my appointments after work as much as possible, and I can't cancel on such short notice anyway. Do you have to have it this weekend?"

"Yes. I've been waiting for the background to dry, and I want to start blocking in some details ... This sucks. I'll probably *never* see you after the baby's born ..."

"*Caitlyn!*" I could tell my mom was mad, but I didn't care anymore.

That's when Tyler stepped in and offered to pick me up after school.

"That would be awesome," I told him. "It's nice to know that *somebody* cares about me!" I shot my mother a dirty look.

"You know I'll always be there for you," he said. "And for your family too, if they need help."

Mom brightened, even though it was obvious to me that he was being a total suck-up.

"Do you want us to pick up some dinner on the way home?" he asked. "Since it sounds like you'll be late getting in ..."

"Great idea!" my mom said. She reached into her purse and pulled out a wad of money. "But why don't the two of you stop for something to eat – we likely won't be home until well after seven. We'll eat later."

Tyler raised his eyebrows, and looked at me from across the table, and I knew perfectly well what he was thinking – that we'd have the place to ourselves for at least three hours after school. It would be a good time for us to be alone together without having to skip class.

Since I was spending so much time with Tyler, I didn't get to see Ashley very much. It seemed like, the more time I spent with Tyler, the more she suddenly wanted me to keep her company. Brandon usually had to do homework and go to his part-time job after football practice, and they didn't spend many evenings together. Tyler practiced a lot too, and he also worked, but we'd meet up afterward when we couldn't cut classes and spend the afternoons together. I didn't have any spare time for Ashley, because when I wasn't with Tyler, I was trying to catch up on whatever schoolwork I'd missed.

Finally, one afternoon, our school's football team played Tyler's, and Ashley and I got to sit together in the stands, just like old times. It was good to talk without the guys around.

I was still trying to keep my relationship with Tyler private, but I decided it was time to tell her about my mom. By that point, I'd been keeping it a secret for months. She was quiet while I explained about the fertility treatments, and how happy my mom was to finally be giving me a brother or sister.

"How come you never told me about this?" Ashley asked. I could see by the look on her face that she was hurt.

"I don't know – I guess I just didn't feel ready," I said. "Plus, there was always a chance something could go wrong," I added feebly.

"Does Tyler know?"

"That's different."

"No it's not. You used to tell me everything," she said.

"So did you."

"I still do," she retorted. "*You're* the one who got all secretive, once you started sneaking around with your new boyfriend."

"We don't sneak around!"

"You do too! I know you cut class together all the time. And he told Brandon he comes over sometimes at night. And don't think every girl in our class hasn't seen those disgusting hickies all over your boobs when we change for gym!"

I felt myself flush all over when she mentioned the hickies. There *had* been quite a few of them, and when I'd asked Tyler to stop marking up my neck, he'd worked his way down lower, which seemed better, because I figured then nobody had to know. I guess I hadn't been as careful in the change room as I'd thought.

"Tyler and I love each other, and we have a mature relationship, and I would think you'd understand what it's like when you first start going out with someone. I didn't see very much of you when you and Brandon first got together, and *you* still only want to hang out with me when *he's* busy! Anyway, Tyler has nothing to do with me not telling you about my mom. Like I said, I just didn't feel like sharing it," I told her.

"I'm worried about you, is all," she said.

"Why?"

"I don't know – I just have a bad feeling. Like you're not as happy as you claim to be."

"Why would you say I'm not happy?"

"Just little things, I guess. Like the hickies. And you don't smile that much, or tell me anything important about the two of you."

"I told you we were in love, but you didn't take me seriously."

"I know, and I'm sorry about that. But that's one of the things that has me worried – you seem so serious about each other already. You're always distracted because you have to rush off to meet Tyler, or finish some assignment you missed when you skipped class to be with him ..."

"So? None of that means I'm not happy. I *am* happy, okay? I'm happy with Tyler. We're happy with each other."

"Okay," she nodded, and looked down at the ground. "You don't seem happy about the baby, though."

"*That's* true," I agreed. "I'm having a lot of trouble getting used to it, and it's not even here yet."

"Aren't you at least happy for your mom and Mike, because they've wanted a baby for such a long time?" she asked, looking up and meeting my eyes.

"Honestly? No," I admitted.

"You've changed," she whispered, looking away again.

"So have you."

We were quiet for a minute. Then I decided to call a truce.

"I don't want to fight, Ashley. Can't we just get along and be happy for each other, like we used to? Before the guys? Maybe if you knew Tyler better you'd understand why I love him so much. We could double-date or something this weekend."

"I guess."

"You can sleep over – it'll be like old times. And I promise to tell you everything that's going on with Tyler and me," I said.

"I'd like that," she agreed.

Chapter 12

*a*shley and I were walking to the bus stop after the game, when a school bus stopped beside us. The door opened, and I saw that Tyler was standing in the doorway – it was his team bus, full of muddy, sweaty football players, all in a great mood, having beat our team 21–6.

"Hop in!" he said. "Coach said it's all right. I'll drive you ladies home from the school."

I was all set to accept a ride, but Ashley didn't look so sure.

"Come on," I said.

"No, that's okay. I'll take the city bus."

"Why? They're going back downtown anyway. Let's go – it'll be fun!" I coaxed.

"Go ahead without me, if you want," she said. "I just

don't feel like it."

I didn't know what her problem was, but I didn't want to upset her again after we'd just made up, so I decided it was best not to go with the guys.

"We're just going to walk down to the city bus, and we'll meet you back at the school like we'd planned," I told him. "Unless you really want me to come along?" I added, seeing that he was disappointed.

"No. It's fine. Whatever," he said.

At that, the bus driver shut the door, and the bus drove off. But the look on Tyler's face gave me a funny feeling in my stomach, and I knew that I should have gone.

Ashley and I caught the city bus.

"Why didn't you want to go with them?" I asked.

"I don't know ... it was a bus full of guys we don't know ... it seemed weird."

"We know Tyler!"

"So you can see him later, right?"

I knew I could – and would – see Tyler later, but I wasn't sure that he'd still be in a good mood. Of course, I didn't admit this to Ashley.

On the way home, she seemed more like her old self – talking about the upcoming weekend, where we'd go with the guys, what kind of snacks we should have for our sleepover. I tried to concentrate on what she was saying, but my thoughts kept drifting back to the look on Tyler's face when I'd said we weren't getting on the bus with him.

When I caught up with Tyler afterward, he was furious.

"Where the hell do you get off embarrassing me like that in front of my team?" he fumed. "I made the coach stop the bus, I offered you a ride, and you turned me down with all the guys there. Do you have any idea how humiliating it is when your own girlfriend doesn't want to be seen with you?"

"It wasn't like that," I tried to explain. "Ashley just didn't feel like being around all the guys, and I didn't want her to be mad at me."

"Well, from where I sit, it looks like I tried to do a nice thing for you, and I got snubbed in front of the team. You really should start thinking about me once in a while," he said.

Once again, I found myself unable to express my thoughts and explain to him that I *had* been thinking about him. That I always was. He wouldn't believe that I'd wanted to go with him on the bus, because I hadn't done it. And if I told him I'd spent the whole trip home with Ashley worried about his reaction, he'd be mad at me for assuming that he was going to be upset. It was nice to feel closer to Ashley again, but it was hard having Tyler mad at me. I wished I'd just gotten on the bus.

That weekend, we all went out to the school dance together. Tyler and Brandon had an early city-wide football tournament the next morning, so they dropped Ashley and me off at my place.

At first, it was just like old times. We did each other's hair and makeup, ate popcorn, and watched a movie, the way we used to. But after we'd turned out the lights, we started talking, and I realized how much things had changed.

"Your mom's really starting to show," Ashley commented.

"I know. It's weird to think she's going to have a baby soon. She made me go shopping with her for maternity underwear," I said.

"What's that?"

"You know – special underwear for when you're pregnant, and after you have the baby."

"They have that?" she asked.

"Yeah – stretchy panties that fit over her stomach. They are, like, *huge*! And also some bras with fold-down flaps on them so she can breastfeed the baby without having to take it off," I explained.

"Gross."

"I know. And it was so embarrassing having to shop for it with my mother! There were all these cute little matching bra and panty sets in the lingerie department, but I didn't even want to look at them, in case she asked me why." This was the closest I'd been in a long time to talking with Ashley about anything important, and it felt good.

"Even if you bought some of that stuff when she wasn't with you, she'd still see it in your laundry, you know," she giggled.

"I know."

We were silent for a minute, and then she whispered, "Sometimes I think I'm going too far with Brandon."

"Sometimes I feel the same way with Tyler!" I was so relieved to have her say out loud what I'd been thinking and worrying about, but had been way too embarrassed to bring up.

"Really?" she said. "Because lately, when we're, like, on the couch or whatever, we've actually been *lying down*, with him, like, on top of me. You know?"

"Mmm hmm," I agreed, thinking about all the times I'd been to Tyler's house over lunch, when I should have been working on my painting.

"... and one time," she continued, "he took my hand, and I thought he was putting it on his thigh, but it turned out it was, umm, higher up, and I was just totally freaked out."

And just like that, the close feeling was gone again.

I understood exactly what she meant about the lying down, and I understood exactly what she meant about ending up with her hand up higher than his thigh, and I remembered how it had freaked me out the first time.

But I also knew, from the tone of her voice, that Ashley and Brandon hadn't gone nearly as far as Tyler and I, and that if I told her about how sometimes we hardly even had any clothes on while we were making out, or about how many times my hand had been there, or especially about what he asked me to do with it when it was, she wouldn't understand. And I was afraid she'd call me a slut again, maybe this time for real and not in a joking voice, because Tyler and I had only been going out for a few months, and she'd been with Brandon for almost a year.

So I just changed the subject.

It hurt that I couldn't even talk to my best friend anymore about my relationship.

Chapter 13

Just as I began to feel myself drifting away from Ashley, my artistic talent seemed to have abandoned me too.

My portrait wasn't going well. I had started with the background, filling it in with muted shades of aqua and purple: cool colors that would complement my red hair and fair complexion. I'd waited for the background to dry a bit before I began working on the face and body. I'd sketched in a few rough details – facial features, the drape of my clothes – but I was having trouble with the expression. I couldn't quite get my lips to look like they were smiling – the expression changed from looking stern, to pained, to slightly psychotic (Conner's words), depending on what I tried, but somehow I just couldn't get it right no matter what I did.

It was unusual for me to have so much trouble with realism, and I was frustrated.

Mrs. Van der Straeten tried to coach me through it.

"You're thinking about it too much," she said. "Leave it for now, finish the background, and don't worry about the expression until one day when you're totally relaxed. Sometimes when we try too hard to make something the way we want it, it ends up being something we *don't* want. It'll come to you, you'll see."

Conner's picture was coming along much better than mine. He never worried about getting things right – he just went ahead and did them. That's why he changed his hair color so much. He had confidence in his talent, so much so that he didn't care what anybody thought. Ever.

His portrait wasn't even close to being realistic, and it didn't look anything like him, but it wasn't supposed to, because that was the way he was creating it.

Conner was doing a sculptural collage to make up a whole image. He'd searched for all kinds of little things that meant something to him, and put them together to create his picture. There were green candies for the colored parts of his eyes, some fur off his cat for eyebrows, and guitar picks for ears. I knew it took a lot of talent to come up with so many ideas for one project the way Conner had, and I was jealous.

Apart from the fact that Conner felt free to experiment while I was stuck in realistic limbo, he also had a lot more done than me, because I had missed so many lunch sessions going out with Tyler.

"So what do you see in this guy?" he asked me one day, as we worked together.

"What guy? The guy in your portrait?"

"*No* – the guy in the portrait is me. I know what you see in me – talent, brains, and of course my winning good looks." He grinned at me. "*Your* guy."

"Who – Tyler?"

"Yeah – your boyfriend. What makes him so wonderful that you want to be with him all the time?" he asked.

"I don't know ... he's gorgeous, and he loves me ..." I started.

"... and?"

"... and I just like being with him," I said.

"And is it just like you pictured the man of your dreams would be? Is he everything you ever hoped for in a boyfriend?"

"Well, not exactly," I started, thinking of how jealous he'd been about my sketches of David, and about what had happened afterward. But I didn't want to share that part of the relationship with Conner, so I added, "He's *more* than I hoped for in a boyfriend."

Conner shrugged. "I guess you're lucky to have someone like that for your first boyfriend, then. *My* first girlfriend was Terry Jinx – remember her? Gorgeous. I knew she was going to dump me for someone better looking as soon as she got a chance."

"With an attitude like that, no wonder!" I said. "And I don't call him my *first* boyfriend, because that sounds like I plan to break up with him someday, and have other boyfriends later."

"Don't you think there's a very good possibility of that happening?" he asked. "I mean, you are only fifteen – it's not like you're ready to get married or anything!"

By this time, Conner had put down his paintbrush, and was leaning across the table with his hands folded together in front of him. It was such an unusual pose for him, looking so serious with his wild jewelry and crazy hair, that for a moment I had a funny urge to paint him like that.

I thought about what he was saying, and what it would be like to marry Tyler. I had put a lot of effort into staying together with him, but I wasn't sure what it *would* be like to be together forever. He'd probably be a lot less jealous later, if we were married, and everything would be easier if he wasn't jealous all the time.

Plus, it kind of sounded romantic to think about staying together always, and getting married right after college or something. But I couldn't quite see myself married to Tyler. Not yet, anyway. I gave Conner a look that told him not to be an idiot.

"Of course I'm not going to get married right now. Like you said, I'm only fifteen!"

Conner opened his mouth, and it looked as if he were going to say something else, but thought better of it.

Chapter 14

*a*t the end of September, my parents found out that the baby was a girl, and they immediately started phoning all their friends to share the news.

I sent an instant message to Tyler.

Sorry I can't call you right now – turns out the baby's a girl, and Mom and Mike are totally hogging the phone to let everyone know. Instant message me, OK?

It didn't take long for him to pop up.

Want me to come over? he typed.

Always!

Twenty minutes later, he was ringing the doorbell. He'd brought flowers for my mom, and one of those big, shiny balloons that says, "It's a girl!"

My mom giggled like a little kid when she saw

the gifts.

"What a charmer you are, Tyler! My own husband didn't even think to get me flowers!"

"Oh, I thought about it ... I'm just trying to save up some money to pay for this kid!" Mike said.

"You don't seem very excited about your little sister," Tyler said later, when we were alone.

"I'm not ... I mean, I guess it'll be better than having a little brother around, but at least then I still would've been the only girl – something to make me special in the family, you know? Now I don't even have that."

"You're special."

"She will be too. And she'll be little, which usually means cuter. And then what have I got?" I felt selfish saying it out loud.

"You'll always be the oldest."

"I'll always be my *mom's* oldest – this one is probably going to be Mike's oldest, youngest, and only. *That* makes her triple special. Plus, they totally wanted her."

"*I* totally want *you*," he said, wrapping his arms around me, and nuzzling his lips into the back of my neck.

"You know," I went on, "when Mom told me tonight that it was going to be a girl, her eyes lit up, and she looked so happy. Then she pulled out this little pink teddy bear she'd picked up on her way home. And I said, 'What was the first thing you bought for me, when you found out about me?' And she got this really guilty look, like she didn't want to think about it, and she said, 'Oh, Caitlyn, that was a long time ago. I'm not even sure they offered to tell me what the ultrasound said, so I didn't know if you were going to be a girl or a boy.' So then I said, 'Okay, but you must have bought *something* when you found out you were expecting me – what was it?' And she said, 'Honestly, honey, I was in such a state of shock that I really don't remember ... your Aunt Caroline bought you a nice blanket, though, to bring you home from the hospital in ...'

"So my own mother admitted to me that she was in such a state of shock when she got pregnant, she couldn't even buy me a teddy bear. You can bet she didn't spend all night on the phone telling everyone she knew, either!" I sniffed.

"So what?" Tyler said. "You're beautiful, and talented, and wonderful, and even if you were a bit of a shock at the time, I'm sure your mother loves you uncondibionally now ..."

"Not as much as she's going to love the new baby," I said, as tears came to my eyes. "You know how much money it was for the fertility treatments? A *ton*. And they extended the mortgage on the house. They haven't said anything yet, but I don't know if there's going to be enough money for me to go to college in a few years, and I always thought it would be kind of fun to spend a year in France – you know, studying all the great artists – but now I don't know if that will ever happen, because they went and used up so much money to basically *buy* me a little sister I never wanted in the first place. A little sister who's totally messing everything up already."

"You'll just have to get rich and famous all by yourself, then," Tyler said. "As an artist," he said, as he kissed my hands, "... or a model ..." He kissed my cheeks. "... or a porn star ..." He kissed my mouth.

"Porn star?"

"Just trying to make you smile, Caitlyn."

"You always make me smile," I told him. "I don't know what I'd do without you."

I still needed to do a project about an artist, and I hadn't even started it yet.

"Who are you working on for your biography?" I asked Conner.

"Diane Arbus," he said.

"Who?"

"Diane Arbus. It's pronounced 'Dee-ann,' but

spelled D-I-A-N-E – you know, like Diane."

"I thought we were supposed to do someone famous?" I asked.

"We are."

"But I've never heard of her."

"There are probably lots of famous people you've never heard of."

"Was she a painter?

"No – a photographer. She used to follow sideshows around, taking pictures of fire-eaters, dog-faced boys – you know, freaks."

"Is she still alive? We're going to have our very own little test-tube mutant at my house soon," I said. "Maybe she'd like to take some pictures."

"Sorry – she's dead. Anyway, it's interesting. Who are you doing?"

"I don't know yet. Goldie the Second has me thinking about Matisse, because of his famous goldfish painting. It's pretty cool."

"Still, neo-impressionism? Are you up for something that's not realistic?" he asked.

"I don't know. Maybe," I shrugged, embarrassed that Conner already knew more about Matisse than I did.

"He painted a lot of fruit too, you know," he said.

"So?"

"So I don't think fruit is your thing – even if goldfish are."

"Are freaks *your* thing?"

"I'm still friends with *you*, aren't I?" he asked, raising one eyebrow, and leaning forward on both elbows.

"What's that supposed to mean?"

"Nothing. I'm just kidding around. Anyway, didn't you say you got an art book for your birthday? There must be someone in there you could research."

I felt a bit guilty thinking about the art book. I'd been so busy with Tyler, and so happy about getting Goldie the Second, I hadn't really taken any time to look through it.

That night, at home, I started leafing through the artists in the book. There were a lot of the painters that everyone's heard of – Picasso, Monet, Van Gogh. Matisse was there too. Conner was right – he painted a lot of fruit. And it wasn't realistic, so as much as I appreciated his stuff, I couldn't really relate to it. I was also starting to worry that I wouldn't have enough time to put into the project, so I figured I might have better luck doing someone a little less well-known to high school students – an artist Mrs. Van der Straeten didn't have to read about year after year, so she wouldn't be as critical if I missed something. I chose a French sculptor named Camille Claudel. Her work was very realistic, like mine;

and from what I'd seen when I was glancing through her biographical information, she'd been almost as famous for one of her love affairs as she was for her art. I liked that – the idea that she was an artist and a romantic, and that she could be remembered for both.

Chapter 15

By early October, Tyler and I were fooling around so much that half the time we didn't even bother turning on the TV anymore, because we both knew why we were there. If his parents were going to be home, we'd stay in the car and park somewhere. I knew he was sexually frustrated, but I didn't actually plan to go all the way with Tyler the first time it happened.

We'd already been making out for a couple of hours. "Just let me try for a minute," he begged. "I promise I won't stay in."

I really wanted to know what it would be like, and it honestly didn't seem like that big a leap from everything else we'd been doing – but I wasn't exactly sure, because of the worries I couldn't name, and the fact that it still seemed kind of soon.

"Not yet," I told him.

"... But I love you so much ..."

"I know, I love you too, it's just that ..."

"It's just that you're such a tease!" he said, flipping me over onto my back, and climbing on top of me.

"Tyler!" I tried to wriggle free, but he had my arms up over my head, and he was holding onto my wrists.

"You know you want to," he said, kissing me hard on the mouth, and bringing himself closer to me.

"Yes, but I ..."

"Yeah, so just lie back and enjoy it," he murmured. *"Please."*

And just like that, I lost my virginity. It was all over really fast. It kind of hurt when he forced it in, but there was hardly any blood or anything, like I'd heard there could be. He seemed really happy afterwards, and he kept saying things like "thank you," and "I love you so much." I knew he was happy, because it was something *he'd* wanted to do. I'd been *thinking* about possibly sleeping with him, but even though I'd thought about it, I hadn't really expected that it would happen that way, and I started to cry even though he was holding me, and saying sweet things to me.

I went back home that night, and had the weekly family dinner with my parents just as if nothing had happened. I even tried to tell myself that nothing *had* happened – that it wasn't a big deal, because we loved each other, so everything was going to be just fine. Underneath the rationalizations, though, I was worried, because we hadn't used anything, and I didn't want to end up like my mother.

And the next week, I missed my period.

Even though I'd spent the first part of my life thinking things like, *"Why would I want a period? Who needs the hassle?"* and, *"It's great to be able to have a baby someday, but why do I have to put up with the cramps and everything for, like, forty years, just so I can get pregnant once or twice?"* I started to change my thinking that week into things like, *"Where are you, period? Hurry up! Please, please, start!"* For the first time ever, I desperately wanted it – and it wasn't coming.

I was making sure Tyler and I didn't have any chances to be alone, because I didn't want it to happen like that again.

We hadn't talked about it, either. Even though we were at a point where he'd seen every part of my body, there were still things we didn't talk about, which is why, when I started to think I might be pregnant, I just couldn't say it out loud. Because I was nervous about discussing it with him in person, I waited until I knew he was online, and then I sent him an instant message.

I'm late.

For wut?

U no!!!! LATE!!!!

U R?

2 days.

Not 2 much

I'm never late, I typed.

O. Wut now? he answered.

I don't know.

U should have been on the pill or sumthing a long time ago, he typed.

I didn't plan it.

U must have had some idea becuz U R so hot!!!

I still didn't plan it!!!! I was starting to get defensive, thinking about how it had happened. *U should have had a rubber or something!!!*

Let's not fight, OK? U R probly fine. I'll get sumthing for next time, he reassured me.

I can't talk now. I have to get caught up on my art project.

I really needed a distraction. I'd started taking notes on Camille Claudel from the book my mom had given me for my birthday. She was born in Champagne, France. She was one of only a few girls allowed to go to art school at the time. Her parents didn't want her to be an artist. She started working with the great sculptor Auguste Rodin when she was 17 – and she started sleeping with him soon after. Who knew a school project could be so racy? I wasn't sure if that was the kind of information Mrs. Van der Straeten wanted, so I looked up "Camille Claudel" on the Internet to see what else I could find out about her.

Unfortunately, instead of distracting me from my period-less state, it made things worse. One site said that Camille and Auguste had as many as four children together, but they just kept sending them to orphanages because he wouldn't leave his other lover, and she couldn't keep them as a single mother in the late 1800's. I hated to think about what my life would have been like if my mom hadn't been able to keep me. And as much as I wasn't ready for it, I couldn't imagine sending my baby, if I was having one, to an orphanage. But at least Tyler didn't have another lover, and I didn't have to share him with anyone, like Camille had to share Auguste.

Chapter 16

*a*s it turned out, I wasn't pregnant after all.

"I never want to go through that again," I said.

"Me either."

We were in Tyler's room, after school.

"... And I don't know how my mom did it – you know, when she was pregnant with me? She must have been freaking out. No wonder she didn't buy me a teddy bear!"

"I would have bought a teddy bear if you'd been pregnant."

"You would have?"

"Sure – it would have been our kid, right?"

"You know, my own father didn't even hang around when Mom got pregnant with me. And the only thing he ever bought me was that fish ..."

"I already bought you a fish."

"I know ... and you know what's weird? Even though I really wanted a puppy, I sort of love Goldie the Second, in a bizarre, as-much-as-you-can-love-a-slimy-thing-that-doesn't-want-you-to-touch-it kind of way."

"Mmm ..." he said. "Kind of like how you love me? Except I'm not slimy, and I very much want you to touch me?"

"Kind of like that," I said, kissing him on the lips.

"How much do you love me?" he asked.

"You know how much."

"I'm glad. I was afraid you were mad ... you know ... about what happened."

"I don't want to talk about that," I told him. And it was true. It was all I'd been thinking about for a week. I couldn't believe I'd had unprotected sex. I couldn't believe I'd had sex at all.

As Tyler held me, I tried to push away the negative thoughts, and come up with good ones. I thought about how, as scared as I'd been that I might have gotten pregnant, he'd sort of been there for me, and he hadn't bailed on me as my father had done to my mom. The fact that he'd stuck it out made me feel a bit better about the whole thing, even though none of it had been the way I'd wanted it to be.

"Good. I don't want to talk either," he said. "And I got something, so we won't have to worry anymore." He reached into his dresser drawer and pulled out a box of condoms.

"I don't know ..." I started to protest.

"We love each other, right?"

"Yes ..."

"So that makes it okay. Besides – we've already done it once. There's nothing holding us back anymore. I love you so much ..." he murmured, slipping his hand up under my sweater.

Two weeks into October, when it seemed as if things were finally settling down again, and I was growing more secure about Tyler, the school mailed out interim reports, and my parents found out the truth about how things were going.

"Seven absences?" My mom looked at me in disbelief. "You've only been in school for six weeks!"

Nobody called home when I was absent from school because Tyler either wrote notes or phoned the school to pretend he was Mike, but we hadn't counted on the school keeping track and putting it on the report. We were busted.

"That might not be exactly right ..." I tried to think up a lie that my mom wouldn't be able to check up on.

"And two 'D's'? You've always been an 'A' student. What's going on here?"

"Math and history are really hard this semester. I told you that." Even I hadn't realized my grades had slipped that much. I bit my lip and looked at the ground.

"I still have a 'B' in art," I added, trying to keep her off the topic of the absences.

She shook her head. "You and I both know that you could get an 'A' in art if you worked blindfolded while standing on your head – you're that talented. But I also think we both have to acknowledge that you and Tyler are spending far too much time together, and that has to be why your grades are slipping."

"No, Mom – it's not his fault. He *helps* me with math, because he's already taken all that stuff."

"Mike has already told me he'd love to help you with that. History too."

"I don't want Mike's help."

"I'm sorry, honey, but we're going to have to restrict you and Tyler to just seeing each other on weekends until you get your grades back up."

"But I told you, it's not his fault. Just give me another chance – I'll work so much harder. Please."

"Caitlyn, I know I've been distracted because of the

baby, but you're still my biggest priority, and I can't have you jeopardize your chances of getting into a good college because of your first crush."

"It's not a crush!" I said angrily.

"Oh, honey, I know. It *feels* like so much more than a crush right now, but you still have to be careful, and think about your future."

"Like you did when you were going out with my real father?"

She didn't take the bait. "We're not talking about me. We're talking about you," she said gently.

"How long am I grounded for?" I asked.

"You're not grounded, but let's make it twenty-minute phone calls and 'weekend-only' dates for a month, and if you bring your grades back up, we'll renegotiate."

I knew there was no point in arguing with her at that point, and I didn't want to draw her attention back to the absences, so I mumbled something about studying, and took off to my room.

I was worried about how Tyler would react to the news that we could only see each other on weekends, because spending time together was so important to him. I decided to send him an instant message to give him the bad news.

Interim reports came out and I can't c u on weeknites

now, I typed.

Why?

U distract me

u distract me 2!

I have 2 d's

that's wut I luv about your boobs! he joked.

ha ha u know I'm not even close 2 that. I mean on my report card.

R your parents really mad? he asked.

could be worse – i can call u later for 20 min. ok?

ok luv u

luv u 2

wish I didn't have 2 wait for Sat.

I no, I wrote.

I went to sleep that night looking forward to Saturday, but I was also secretly relieved that I wouldn't have to worry about Tyler wanting to have sex with me again until then.

Chapter 17

Tyler thought that I should get a belly ring.

The idea came up on the second night of "twenty-minute phone conversations only." All I said was that I thought belly rings looked sort of cool, and – wham! – just like that, he was telling me I should totally go for it.

I'd never really thought of myself as belly ring material – plus, I didn't really understand why he wanted me to have it so badly, since he was jealous all the time anyway, and belly rings attract attention. It did sound kind of intriguing, though.

I mentioned the idea at dinner the next night.

"No way," Mike said.

"I agree," my mother said. "Navel piercing can be very dangerous, and it leaves a scar if you change your mind. Did you know you have to take them out when you get pregnant?" she said, patting her own baby bulge.

My face burned, and I wondered what my mother knew about Tyler and I.

"I'm not pregnant," I told them.

"Well of course you're not *now*, sweetie. I mean later, when you're married, and you're ready to have children. You can't have a belly ring *then*, so getting one *now* would be pretty silly."

Seeing Tyler wasn't a good idea, getting a belly ring was "silly." It seemed as if everything I wanted to do was a bad idea, as far as my parents were concerned.

Tyler said almost the same thing that night on the phone. "So? Why can't you just take it out someday when we're ready to have kids?" Even after the pregnancy scare, I realized that he was looking into the future, and seeing me as the mother of his children. A little shiver ran up my spine when I thought about it.

"I guess I could – except they won't let me get it done, so it doesn't matter."

"Do it anyway," he urged. "It would be so sexy on you. I get hot just thinking about it."

"You mean, go against my parents and get my belly button pierced anyway?"

"Why not? It's *your* body, right? You don't tell them about everything you do."

I knew he was talking about sex. And he was right. They wouldn't have wanted me to do that either, but really it wasn't up to them. It was up to me and Tyler, and we'd sort of decided together. It wasn't exactly the way I'd pictured it, but that didn't mean I couldn't make other decisions for myself.

We decided to go downtown on the weekend, when we could finally be together again, and get the piercing done.

Tyler wrote a note and signed it with Mike's name, just as we did at school, because I was under eighteen and couldn't get the piercing done without a parent's permission.

The girl who did it had piercings everywhere – in her earlobes, at the top of her ear in the cartilage part, on her nose, her lip, and her eyebrow.

"Do you have a belly ring too?" I asked her, as she swabbed my stomach with topical anesthetic.

"Uh huh. Right here, see?" She lifted her shirt up just a bit so I could see the silver ring that went in just above her belly button and came out through the center of it.

"Does it hurt a lot?" I asked. I was starting to have doubts that it was a good idea, and I wondered whether Tyler would change his mind too if she said it was painful.

"Nah – it's not much worse than having your ears done. Anyway, I'm going to use anesthetic – they don't do that for ear piercing, so you might feel it even less," she said.

"Do you use the same kind of gun as they use on your ears?" I asked, as she finished swabbing the area, and it started to get numb.

"Nope ..." By this time, she'd clamped the area around my bellybutton with tong-type things. "We use this big needle." Then she pulled out a needle that was as long as my hand, and before I had a chance to chicken out, she pierced through my skin and inserted a ring.

It looked amazing. Tyler put his arms around me, and gave me a long, deep kiss right there in the store.

"That looks so hot!" he whispered in my ear, as the girl covered my new ring with a bandage.

I was glad I'd had it done, but by the time we got out to the car, the area around the bandage was starting to turn red and swell up a bit, and even though the freezing was still working, it felt uncomfortable when I put my seatbelt on, so I had to ride home without a belt.

The girl who did the piercing gave me a pile of instructions to follow so I wouldn't get one of those infections my mom had warned me about. *Swab it with alcohol. Take saltwater baths. Wear loose clothing. Don't go swimming for a few weeks, and when you do go, make sure it's a well-chlorinated pool.*

Because of the risk that it could close up, I couldn't take the ring out even for a few hours until it was completely healed – which the brochure said could be between four months and *two years*. I didn't know how I was going to hide it from my parents for that long. But I tried not to get too close when my mom hugged me goodnight.

As the anesthetic began to wear off, it started to hurt a bit. Not bad, but kind of like I'd cut myself and been punched in the gut all at once.

I followed the instructions to the letter, with rubbing alcohol and everything, but a couple of days after I'd had it done, it started to get redder and hurt a lot more. I took some Aspirin, and told my mom I had a headache when she suggested going for a walk together. A few days after that, I noticed that there was some liquid oozing out of it. It was kind of greenish yellow, and it smelled bad. Worst of all, I hurt all over – it wasn't just the piercing that ached, but my whole body. I told my mom I had the flu.

Mike told her to stay away from me – my own mother! He was afraid she'd catch the flu from me and hurt the baby. For once, my mom stood up for me instead of the baby, and insisted on feeling my forehead.

"You're burning up. You've got a really high fever!"

"I'll be okay ..." I said.

"No, I think you need to see the doctor," she insisted.

I tried to protest, but she wouldn't listen, and the next thing I knew, I was in the doctor's office. My mom followed me right in.

"Um, Mom? Do you think maybe I could see the doctor alone?" I asked.

"Why do you want to see her alone?"

"I don't know. It's just that it's kind of embarrassing to get undressed in front of you and everything ..." By this time, I was feeling so weak and sick all over that it was hard for me to even argue, but she agreed, and sat down in the waiting room while a nurse helped me to the examination room.

Dr. Mills had been my doctor for as long as I could remember.

"What seems to be the problem?" she asked as I entered. "It says here you've got the flu?"

"I guess so ..." I told her.

"Well, let's see what we've got." She put a thermometer in my ear, agreed with my mother that my temperature was really high, and began asking questions about how long I'd been feeling this way.

"Headache? Body ache? Nausea? Any pain? When did it start?"

I was able to answer every question perfectly

honestly, without having to reveal my secret, until she said, "Okay, lie down. I need to feel your abdomen and make sure we're not looking at appendicitis."

I leaned back onto the table, and lifted my shirt – and then she saw it. The swollen red mess that used to be my belly button.

"Is that a new belly ring?"

"Uh-huh."

"Let me guess: you had it done a few days ago? Right before your symptoms started?"

"Yes ..."

"Why didn't you tell me right away?"

"I don't know ... I didn't think I could feel so awful all over from something so small. And I did everything they told me to do ..."

"Sometimes even when you take all the precautions, things can go wrong."

"I thought maybe I really did have the flu or something," I protested.

"A smart girl like you?"

"... and ... my mom doesn't know," I confessed.

"About the belly ring?"

"Right. Please don't say anything about it. She's so grumpy already, with her being pregnant and everything, she'll blame my boyfriend, and I'll be grounded forever."

"What does your boyfriend have to do with it?"

"Well, nothing, really. I mean, it was sort of his idea originally, but I wanted to do it too, and when I asked, Mom said 'no,' just because she doesn't like him that much, and she thinks he has too much influence on me, so I know she'll blame him again."

"Why does she think he has too much influence on you?"

"Because I'm not a little kid anymore, and I don't do every little thing that she wants."

"How long have you been with your boyfriend?"

"A couple of months."

"Are you sexually active?"

"What?"

"You and your boyfriend – are you having sex?"

"No," I lied.

"The reason I ask," she said, as she took out her prescription pad and began to write, "is because a number of girls your age are sexually active, and regardless of whether or not I think it's a good idea, I would rather you were up front about it now so we can talk about contraception, and STDs, and taking care of your body. Because right now you are *very* sick, and I suspect that if you had been honest with your mother about the piercing a lot of the pain you're in could have been avoided. And that pain is nothing compared to the pain of an unplanned pregnancy, or the AIDS virus. So if you need some advice, now is a great time to ask." As she finished her speech, she handed me a prescription.

"What's this?" I asked.

"Some heavy-duty antibiotics. You need to start taking them right away, or you risk blood poisoning, and even death."

"*Death?*"

"Yes."

"Oh. Does it have to come out?" I asked.

"At this point, I'd rather leave it where it is. We don't want to spread the infection by messing around down there," she said.

"Thanks," I murmured, relieved that I'd at least get to keep it for now.

"I *do* need to tell your mother about it," she said, "because you're in a very precarious situation right now, and if the fever doesn't go down in a couple of hours, she's going to have to take you to the emergency room at the hospital."

"*Hospital?*"

"Hospital," she repeated. "So we will invite your mother in to talk about the piercing ... but just the piercing. I am not required by law to answer the questions of parents who request information about their child's sexuality, if the child is over the age of fourteen. It's different in different parts of the country, but if there's anything else you want to talk about today, your privacy is completely assured."

"No thanks, it's okay," I managed to tell her. I still felt sick and weak all over, and all I could think about was how my mother was going to lose it when she heard about the stupid belly ring. I wasn't up for further discussion.

"Okay, then. I'll bring your mom in."

I barely remember the rest of the visit. The doctor told my mom I had something to share with her, my mom went all pale and got sort of crazed looking, and then I showed her my angry red stomach, and she started to cry. Whatever was said after that, the stop at the pharmacy to pick up my prescription, and even the trip home, is a complete blur. I took some of the pills and went to bed, and slept for almost twenty-four hours, waking up only when my mom came in to give me another pill or to take my temperature. A lot of my exhaustion was because I was so sick, but I also think some of it was the relief of having things out in the open. I was finally able to sleep soundly, without fear of my secret being discovered.

Chapter 18

When Mike found out, he was furious.

"How could you do something so stupid and irresponsible?" he railed. "And after your mother and I forbade you. You know your mom's in a delicate state right now, and you risked not only yourself but also your baby sister by putting your mom under so much stress. You're not going to be an only child for much longer, and you'd better start thinking about other people."

As much as he said I'd been stupid and selfish, he also blamed Tyler, saying he was a bad influence on me, and we couldn't see each other anymore. My mom sided with him.

"Caitlyn, I can't tell you how disappointed we are in both you and Tyler," she said.

"Don't blame him! I wanted to get it done," I said feebly.

"Oh, I know it's not entirely his fault, and believe me, I'm going to hold you accountable. But signing the note to let you get the piercing done was illegal. We *could* have him arrested."

I was still too weak to put up much of a fight. "Please don't," was all I could manage.

The next morning, Mike gave me the news. As far as they were concerned, Tyler and I were done. I wasn't allowed to see him, or talk to him on the phone. They wanted me to "get healthy," "concentrate on my schoolwork," "develop some new interests" (which I'm pretty sure meant get a different boyfriend), and "think about my future." In return, they wouldn't press charges against Tyler.

While I was sick, they'd checked in with the school to find out about assignments I'd need to catch up on. By this time, they'd figured out that Tyler was also responsible for all the afternoons I'd missed, so they got Tyler banned from entering the building, and took away my permission to leave school grounds at lunch. They also told the school office that if anyone called or sent a note to cover an absence for me, the school had to double-check by phoning my mom back at her office immediately.

The conditions sucked, but I didn't argue, because I remembered pretty quickly that Mom and Mike aren't that good with technology, and they'd forgotten all about email and instant messaging.

The more they tried to keep me from Tyler, the more determined I became to keep him in my life. I was starting to see that *Tyler* was right: my parents *did* treat me like a little kid. They were blaming everything on him, and they refused to believe that I was capable of making a decision on my own.

I missed a week of school, and even though I was able to use the computer, being cooped up at home sick was especially hard since I was totally grounded from seeing Tyler in person.

Once again, I needed Ashley's help so I could get together with him.

"Cover for me so I can see Tyler after school?" I asked her at lunch on my first day back.

"You're still going out with him?" She sounded surprised.

"Well, duh! Of course I am," I said.

"I thought you said your parents grounded you from seeing him?"

"They did. That's why I need you to cover for me. All you have to do is say I'm in the washroom if my parents call your house, and then call me over at Tyler's so I can phone them back from his place. They think I'm going to your house to get caught up on my schoolwork."

"I don't know ..." she protested.

"I'd do it for you – come to think of it, I *have* done it for you, when you first started going out with Brandon, and you hadn't told your mom yet."

"She's right, Ash," Brandon cut in.

"See?"

"Okay." Ashley still sounded reluctant. I hoped she'd be more convincing if my parents did check up on me.

"You're really stuck on him, aren't you?" Brandon asked.

"More than you know," I told him.

"Is he treating you all right?"

"What do you mean?"

"You know – is he good to you? Does he deserve you?" I was surprised to hear Brandon sounding so concerned about me.

"He doesn't deserve to be treated like crap by my parents, if that's what you mean."

"I know – he told me the belly ring was as much your idea as his. I just wanted to make sure everything else was okay ... you know, because I've known you a lot longer than he has."

I wondered what he was really talking about. I

didn't say much to Ashley when Tyler and I had problems, but I didn't really know if Tyler talked to Brandon, or anybody else, about us. I also didn't know how much detail he went into with other guys about stuff we did. I didn't think he'd be a creep and brag or anything, but Brandon's questioning made me a little uneasy.

"Thanks. I'm good. All I really need is to see the guy I love, because it's been over a week, and I miss him so much. And I can't skip class anymore, because my parents are onto that too. So will you guys cover for me, or not?"

They still seemed hesitant, but they agreed.

Tyler picked me up right after school and took me back to his place. We had a couple of hours before his parents would be home.

"Let's see that belly ring," he said, lifting my shirt gently to take a peek. The bruises had faded to mottled green and yellow, but it was still a really nasty mess.

"Oh – Caitlyn – I am so sorry!" he whispered. "I never wanted anyone or anything to hurt you, and then I let this happen!" He reached out and gently touched my face.

"It wasn't your fault. I wanted it too," I told him. "Anyway, being grounded from you is the thing that hurts me the most."

"Let's just sit together, just like this," he said, wrapping his arms around me. It was one of the nicest times we'd spent together in ages.

Chapter 19

When I got home that night, I felt so relaxed and happy that I thought I should try again to finalize the facial features on my portrait – the mouth still hadn't come out smiling, and the eyes didn't seem right either. Almost everyone who saw it said it was "nice," but usually there was higher praise for my artwork, so I knew it wasn't quite perfect.

It occurred to me, as I struggled with the details, that I'd been looking in the mirror, and maybe seeing myself backwards was the problem: I couldn't really know how I looked when all I ever saw was a reflection. I mentioned it to my parents at dinner when they asked about my schoolwork, and Mike offered to take some digital photographs of me that I could work from.

I tried to model for them the way I pictured my portrait, but every time the flash went off, I blinked, and we ended up with a whole bunch of pictures of my eyelids.

"It looks like you're falling asleep," my mom giggled, as she checked the viewfinder with Mike. "Maybe I need to start tucking you in early every night, like when you were little!"

"At least we've discovered the real reason why you're having trouble painting," Mike joked. "Obviously, it's because you can't keep your eyes open!"

"Well maybe my eyes are closing because I don't want to see the two of you making goo-goo eyes at each other all the time," I teased. "Give me the camera for a minute."

"You're not going to throw it at me, are you?" he asked, with a mischievous look on his face.

"No," I said. "I just want to get a picture of the two of you so I can show my little sister what a weird family she's got."

"It's not a family without you too, Caitlyn," Mike said.

He set up the automatic timer on the camera, then dashed back over to stand with us. The camera clicked and took a perfect photo, with everyone open-eyed and smiling.

Unfortunately, the photos didn't help with my portrait the way I'd hoped.

"I don't know what's wrong with it," I confided to Conner the next day. "I've tried it so many ways – the basic idea is there, and it almost seems right if you don't look too closely, but I just don't feel good about it. It doesn't look like me. Not the way I see myself, anyway. No matter what I try, I can't make it work."

"Maybe you don't see yourself the way other people do," he said.

"What do you mean?"

"You know – like skinny girls who think they need to lose weight, or fat girls who don't realize they're fat – maybe you have a distorted picture of yourself, and that's why you can't put it down on canvas."

"So which am I? A skinny girl who thinks she's fat, or a fat girl who thinks she's skinny?"

"A sad girl who thinks she's happy," he said.

"I *am* happy."

"Then why can't you put a smile on your face?" he said, gesturing to the painting, but looking at me.

"I told you, I don't know – I'm usually so good at things that are realistic," I told him.

"So maybe you're *not* being realistic."

"And maybe *you're* not being helpful."

I tried to smile, to prove him wrong, and so it

wouldn't seem like I was mad at him, but inside I really felt like crying.

Chapter 20

$\mathcal{I}$ actually did cry – out of frustration – several times over the next week, because I missed Tyler so much.

Halloween was coming up, and his school was having a big dance. He had to go because they were fundraising for his football team, but I was still grounded from seeing him.

I'd never had a boyfriend at Halloween before, and I was really afraid that I wouldn't be able to get to the dance, because I'd always wanted to be part of a cute couple costume – the kind that goes together, like a king and queen, or salt and pepper shakers, but better.

I instant-messaged Tyler for ideas a few days before Halloween.

wut do you want 2 wear 4 the dance? we should do a

costume 2gether

like what?

u no – like Superman and Lois Lane or sumthing – u would look good in the tights! I said.

well u would look like my mother in the glasses LOL!!! u should wear something sexy, he wrote.

like Tarzan and Jane?

that's cool! u can swing on my tree anytime! :) !!!

can't wait 2 c u in a loin cloth ;)

u no wut would be better? he said.

wut???

the Flintstones

Fred and Wilma??? I had no idea how that could be better than Tarzan and Jane.

NO – Bamm-Bamm and Pebbles bcuz of your red hair.

Goo goo ga ga!! luv u!!!

luv u 2!

My costume was easy. For my Pebbles outfit, I used some black shorts like a diaper bottom, and I ripped the sleeves off one of Mike's old T-shirts so it hung kind of loose, but sexy and off-the-shoulder. I also tore the bottom off it in that crazy, zig-zaggy way that all the Flintstones have their clothes, and I used fabric paint to add some spots so it would look like animal skin. Finally, I stopped by the pet shop to buy a rubber bone so I could tie my hair up in a ponytail with it. We were going to look so good together.

The problem was, my parents were still being suspicious and overprotective, so they wouldn't agree to let me go out, even though I told them I was just going over to Ashley's.

"How do we know you're not going to meet Tyler as soon as you leave the house?" Mike said.

"I told you, I'm going out with Ashley and Brandon," I said – not exactly a lie, but not exactly an answer to his question, either.

"I'm not sure we're even ready to let you out with Ashley yet," my mom said.

"Come on, Mom! It's Halloween, and I'm already too old for trick-or-treating, and pretty soon I'm going to be too old to dress up for parties too."

"Maybe you should have thought of that before you went behind our backs," she retorted, "and dressed up your navel like a Christmas tree!"

I emailed Tyler: *don't know if i can make it, still working on it, luv u anyway.*

The afternoon before the dance, she still hadn't changed her mind, but she was in a good mood, setting out the jack-o'-lantern, and getting the candy ready by the door.

"You know what?" she said. "I can't wait to have another baby in the house. It's going to be so much fun having a little person around again at Halloween, and at Christmas ..."

I tried again. "Mom, can I at least sleep over at Ashley's, and help give out the candy there?"

"Is Brandon going to be there?"

"No. You said I should spend less time on guys, and more time with Ashley, and this is a perfect opportunity, because you'll know exactly where I am."

Mom sighed. "I wish you'd asked me earlier. I don't have time to take you over there right now."

"Ashley's mom will come and get me." I tried not to scream with excitement. "So does that mean I can go if I get a ride?"

"Okay, but I'm going to check with her when she gets here, to make sure you're not picking anyone else up."

I decided to surprise Tyler, and just show up at the dance without telling him I'd managed to get out of the house.

Ashley rang the bell when she and her mom arrived. She was wearing a wedding dress covered in lace and frills.

"That's an awfully pretty dress for a sleepover, Ashley," my mom said when she saw her.

"It's from my mom's second wedding," Ashley said, twirling around like a ballerina. "And I figured I might as well dress up – you know, for the kids."

"Speaking of your mom, I want to talk to her for a second," my mom said, following us out to the car.

"You're sure it's no trouble for Caitlyn to sleep over?" my mom asked Ashley's mom in the driveway.

"Oh, not at all," she said. "We always enjoy having her over."

"And there won't be any boys over tonight?" Mom asked.

I held my breath, hoping Ashley's mom wouldn't leak any details, but Ashley quickly whispered to me that she had only told her that I was coming for a sleepover.

"Oh no – just the ladies."

"Have a good time, then," Mom said.

As soon as we got to Ashley's, I changed into my Pebbles costume.

Ashley's mother had no idea that I wasn't supposed to go out, so when Brandon phoned and invited us to go out to a dance, just like we'd planned, her mom agreed. Brandon, of course, was dressed like a groom, to go with Ashley's bridal gown. He had a top hat, and tails, and a pair of white gloves. The two of them looked as if they'd fallen off a wedding cake.

I couldn't wait to see my Bamm-Bamm!

The football team's fundraiser, as it turned out, was a kissing booth – a minor detail nobody had mentioned.

Tyler, with his football-player muscles in his Bamm-Bamm loincloth, appeared to be a popular attraction. He was in the booth when we arrived, pecking girls on the cheek for $1.00 apiece. I didn't care so much about the little kisses – and I was sort of proud that he had so many customers – but I was a bit upset that he hadn't told me about it. Still planning to surprise him, I got in line behind a girl in a vampire costume.

When it was Vampire Girl's turn, she slapped down a couple of bills, reached around the back of his head, pulled him toward her, and kissed him long and deep. He didn't push her away. The other football players clapped and cheered.

For a moment, I was frozen. My mouth went totally dry, and I felt like I couldn't breathe. Vampire Girl turned to leave the line, then flipped her head back to smile and wink at Tyler. Her cape swished against my bare legs as she left.

Tyler was still grinning from her kiss when he realized that "Pebbles" was next in line. He stopped smiling, we looked at each other – and I turned and ran. "Caitlyn! *Wait!*" he called after me.

I sat down in the hall and sobbed.

When he found me, he acted as if nothing had happened. "Caitlyn! I'm so glad you came ... I know that looked bad, but I'm really glad you made it here."

"Why? So I could watch you make out with another girl? What – did you think I'd enjoy it?" I cried.

"No, no – it wasn't like that – I swear, I barely know her, and she just put a bunch of money down and said she was going to give me the kiss of death – you now, because she's a vampire – and then she grabbed me ... and if you dump me over this, it really *will* have been the kiss of death, because I'd die without you, Pebbles," he said.

"Why should I believe you?"

"Because it's the truth – look, ask the other guys ..."

Some of the other football players had come out into the hall, and Tyler called out to them. "John – hey – tell my beautiful girlfriend here that I didn't ask for that vampire's tongue, and Pebbles is the only one Bamm-Bamm ever talks about."

"It's true, he never shuts up about you," said a guy dressed like a skeleton. "But just in case, maybe we ought to cool him off with a cold shower, eh, guys?" Three or four of them grabbed Tyler and carried him off into the guys' locker room.

"Where are you taking him?" I followed them in, and saw that they had already turned on the showers and tossed him in.

"Oh look," said the skeleton. "She's come to his rescue. She must need a shower too!"

And before I could protest, they'd dragged me into

the shower as well.

"Let's give these lovebirds some privacy," the skeleton said, as they turned out the lights and backed out the door.

The water, as it turned out, *wasn't* cold. Without saying a word, Tyler reached out, put his arms around my waist, and pressed me up against the wall, his body tight with mine, then kissed me hard on the lips. I'd been so mad and so hurt, but somehow, there in the dark, with the hot, steamy water dripping down my face and my body, even as I thought, *I might be breaking up with him, this might be our last kiss,* I couldn't bring myself to pull away. I drank in the moment, because I couldn't get enough of him.

Chapter 21

"*I* would have thought you'd relate better to Vincent Van Gogh," Conner said when I started to tell him about Camille Claudel the next day in school.

"Van Gogh? Isn't he a little bit overdone and obvious?" I asked.

"But you have so much in common with him – you know, the whole 'tortured lover' thing. Remember how he cut off his left earlobe and delivered it to a woman who refused his affections?"

"That's the most disgusting thing I've ever heard. How could you say I'm anything like that?" I asked.

"You pierced your body for love."

"No, I did it for me – I wanted to do it. It had nothing to do with proving my love."

"I didn't say it had anything to do with *proving* your love, but it's interesting that you should bring that up ..." Conner said. He stopped painting, and looked me straight in the eye.

"Why?"

"Because you're always defending Tyler, and making excuses for him, and I keep wondering why a smart girl like you feels the need to go out with somebody who makes her feel bad all the time."

"I am *not* always defending him, and he does *not* make me feel bad all the time! He can be really sweet."

"When he's not kissing other girls."

"Who told you that? I'm going to kill Ashley," I said. "Anyway, it was a fundraising thing for his team, and he didn't know that girl was going to grab him, and we worked it all out."

"There you go again," he interrupted.

"There I go again what?"

"Defending him," he said. I tried to glare at him, but he'd looked back down at his painting, so I couldn't meet his eyes.

"Every relationship has its ups and downs," I explained, trying not to prove him right by sounding defensive.

"Love should make you feel good, not bad," he said.

This time, it was easy to catch his eye. He was looking right at me, and I'd never seen him so serious.

I thought about Conner's words that night as I worked on my biography project. It was starting to seem that the love affair between Camille and Auguste Rodin wasn't quite as romantic as it had first appeared. They had become lovers when she was only seventeen, but he was already in his forties, which was pretty creepy. And a lot of people said she was *more* talented than Rodin, but he kind of held her back, because she worked on a lot of his projects with him rather than doing her own stuff. Plus, there was the whole complication of him refusing to leave his wife. When he finally broke up with Camille for good, Camille went crazy and destroyed a bunch of her own artwork, and ended up spending the rest of her life in an asylum.

Reading about the depressing details of their relationship made me wonder why she stayed with him as long as she did, and I said so to my mother that night after dinner. Ever since I'd been sick, she'd been having more trouble with the pregnancy, and she was under strict doctor's orders to lie down as much as possible if she wanted to avoid being put on total bed rest. I was still furious with her for banning me from seeing Tyler, but Mike thought it was my fault that she was having problems, because of the stress I'd caused, so I figured the best option I had was to cooperate and keep her company, in hopes that maybe she'd start to trust me again.

"So why do you think Camille did stay with Rodin?" she asked.

"I'm not sure ... her old letters and stuff say that her family didn't approve of Rodin, because he was so much older, and because he was married ... but I don't think we can ever really know what goes on between two people when they're alone together, and in love. Maybe she was learning a lot from him, or maybe he was really sweet to her, but all that's recorded in history is the crap her family said about him."

"Maybe," my mom said. "Or maybe she was just a young girl who thought she'd found true love, but didn't know that it wasn't perfect because she didn't have anything to compare it to. I was a little bit like that, with your father."

"My real dad?" I couldn't believe she was actually bringing him up. She never mentioned him unless I did first.

"Mmm hmmm," she said. "He was sweet, and good to me, and I thought he was perfect – but I didn't know enough about love to realize that he was just Butterscotch

Ripple, and I deserved Heavenly Hash."

"So my father wasn't good enough for you?" I felt like I was going to cry, and I didn't want her to see it on my face.

"No, he wasn't good enough for *us*. He'd promised me the moon and the stars, but when he found out about you, he left. *We* deserved better. *Both* of us."

"And Mike is Heavenly Hash?"

"Yes, Mike is Heavenly Hash," she said with a smile.

"Does that mean the new baby is going to be a perfect little angel?" I asked sarcastically.

"Of course she is," my mom said.

Months of frustration boiled over, and I couldn't stop myself anymore. I turned around, and snapped at my mom and her fat, pregnant belly. "So that's it, then? You wanted an angel, and I'm just leftover Butterscotch Ripple?"

"Caitlyn ..."

"It's okay, Mom. I know she's a 'do-over' – a chance to have the baby you want, with the man you want, at the time you want – a perfectly-planned person – not just a big mistake like me!"

I was really crying now, and didn't care anymore if she saw. It felt good to finally say it to her face. It was such a relief.

My mom grabbed me and hugged me tight. She was

crying too, now, and whispering "no, no ..." over and over again. Mike must have heard me screaming at my mom, because he rushed into the room.

He looked at me with concern for a moment before saying, "Is that what you think, Caitlyn? That you were a mistake?"

"It's not what I *think* – it's the *truth*."

"You were *not* a mistake," my mom said. "Don't you ever think that!"

"In fact, *you're* the reason we want this baby so badly," Mike cut in.

"I know, so you can have one of your own, and love her more."

"You *are* my own – and I could never love her more than I love you, and I am so sorry if anything we've said or done has made you feel like anything less than my own daughter," he continued. "You know what your mom said to me the first time I met her?"

"No ..."

Mom smiled, and continued the story: "I told him not to even bother asking me out unless he could learn to love my little girl, because she was the most important thing in the world to me, and the best thing I'd ever done."

"... and she was right," Mike added. "Which is why we both wanted another baby – because you have brought such joy to our lives, and it has been such a privilege to be your parents."

"You don't look at me and wish I was his daughter?" I asked Mom, pointing at Mike.

"Not for a moment did I ever wish you were anyone but you," she said.

"Even when you saw the mess I made of my stomach?"

"Even then."

Afterwards, when I was alone in my room, I couldn't help thinking about all the classes I'd skipped, and the times I'd sneaked out, and how I'd ended up sleeping with my boyfriend. And I wondered whether my mom would still like me just the way I was if she really knew who I'd become.

Then again, even I was starting to feel like I didn't know who I was anymore.

Chapter 22

*D*espite all of the new things about myself I wasn't sure I liked, one change I did wish for in myself was more imagination.

Mrs. Van der Straeten was trying to get us to move beyond our artistic "comfort zones." We'd been studying "variations on a theme," which means an artist draws the same thing – like maybe a cow – in a whole bunch of different ways. Now she was going to make us try it in class.

"Pick something, and re-create it in three ways," she told us. "As you really see it, as you wish to see it or as it might be, and as others see it."

Conner put up his hand. "Does that include how you might see it if you were madly in love?" The whole class laughed, but Mrs. Van der Straeten was unfazed.

"Absolutely. As the artist, you have to identify your audience, and help them interpret your work by guiding them beyond what they think they see, and towards what you want them to see. If you're madly in love, you're definitely going to see the world differently than someone who's just mad."

As isolating as it was to be grounded from seeing Tyler, I was finding it easier to focus on my schoolwork without having to balance it against spending all my time with him, and I wanted to start the project right away, before I got behind again. Mom and Mike were out shopping for baby furniture, which was perfect, because I'd decided to try and paint the baby again, and I didn't want Mom and Mike to see it. I knew they might not like my version of the baby as much as the one they'd been picturing.

Even though my mom's stomach was huge, and she'd brought home a bunch of ultrasound pictures, I was still having trouble imagining what this little creature might look like. So I dug up some of my own baby pictures to use for reference.

I had to admit – my mom did look happy in every single one of them.

The first baby sketch was the easiest for me. I just did what I'd always done: drew what I saw, making it look like the photo. Simple. As always, it was the imaginary bit that was hard. I didn't even know where to start.

I called Conner.

"Try picturing the baby like a cartoon," he suggested.

"That's the problem – I can't."

"Well, can you break it all into pieces, Picasso style?"

"I tried that too, but then I just want to correct it – put the pieces back where they belong, and make it look perfect."

He was quiet for a minute.

"You know," he said, "just because something looks perfect on paper doesn't mean that it is perfect in real life."

"... but that's my specialty ... making it look perfect ..."

"I know," he said softly, "and I really don't think I'm going to be able to help you until you can let go of that."

I was still mulling over what he'd said when I heard the doorbell ring. It was Tyler – somehow he knew my parents were out.

"They'll *ground me forever* if they catch you here!" I hissed, even as I kissed him and led him downstairs to my room. As much as I had hated being apart from Tyler, everything seemed much more exciting when we did get to see each other.

"What are you working on?" he asked when he saw the drawing on my desk.

"'Variations on a theme,'" I explained, "like I said in my email. My theme is 'the new baby,' but I'm having trouble imagining her as anything different than just a baby."

"Can you make her look evil or something, like if she really is a mutant test-tube monster who doesn't come out right?"

I laughed. "I think that's another way to say what Conner was just describing ... he said to do it like a Picasso, with extra noses and eyeballs in the middle of the forehead, which is kind of evil sounding, if you ask me."

"What do you mean, he was 'just saying it' – is he here?" Tyler looked around the room, as if searching for a hiding spot.

"No – on the phone. I was having trouble coming up with ideas, so I called him."

"Why didn't you call me? Aren't I always supportive of your art?" He sounded hurt.

No, you're not always supportive of my art, I thought. *You destroyed my sketches, and you hit me while we were arguing about it.*

Despite what I was thinking, I didn't want to make him angry when we were finally alone again, so I decided not to say it out loud.

"Yeah, I guess. It's just that Conner's in the class, and he's really good at thinking creatively ..."

"Isn't there anyone *else* in the class you could call?" He was starting to sound angry, so I tried to play it cool.

"I don't know ... why does it matter?"

"I've already told you what I think of that guy. And Brandon says you spend a lot of lunch hours together, now that I can't see you at noon ..."

"Brandon? What does Brandon have to do with anything? Are you using Brandon to spy on me?" Now I was the one getting angry.

"I'm not using him to spy, I just asked him how you spend your time when we can't be together – if you're hanging with Ashley a lot – and he said they don't really see you much because most lunch hours you take off for art class with that Conner guy."

"Because I have to catch up on my assignments!"

I didn't know how to make him see how hard I was trying. I'd been working through almost every lunch hour, trying to get caught up after a week off school, and what seemed like a thousand skipped classes I'd spent with him instead of working on my project, and he was still questioning my loyalty.

"If you're so far behind that you have to hang out with a guy I specifically told you I disapprove of, then maybe you're not as smart as I thought you were."

"What?"

"I think I should go."

"Maybe you should," I retorted.

He picked up a framed picture of the two of us and tossed it across the room, hitting the side of Goldie's tank.

"Leave my fish alone! He didn't do anything to you!" I screamed.

"Your fish? *I* gave him to you. I could take him back right now – and come to think of it, maybe I will." He moved towards the tank.

"Don't you dare!" I flung myself between Tyler and Goldie, and raised my arms to block his reach. He grabbed my arm and twisted it hard. I fell onto the bed, sobbing.

"Caitlyn! Oh my God – are you okay?" he asked.

"No, you hurt me," I said. "You say you love me, but you hurt me."

"I am so sorry," he whispered. "I just wanted you to put your arm down so we could talk – I didn't mean to hurt you!" He stroked my hair and wiped my tears with his fingertips.

"I didn't want you to take Goldie ..." I sniffed. It sounded stupid when I said it out loud.

"I wasn't going to," he said. "I was just upset, that's all. I'm sorry. I shouldn't have said I was going to take him ... he's yours, you know that."

"... and *I'm yours*, and *you* should know *that*," I sniffed.

"I do. You know I just get crazy jealous."

"I can't keep doing this ..." I told him.

"I know. I'm sorry."

He held me, and as we sat together and talked in person for the first time in a long time, I started to feel normal and good again. I tried to keep my mind off of what had happened by telling him in more detail about what was going on at school, and how frustrated I was becoming with art class, not only with independent study, but also with the assigned "variations" project.

Amazingly, Tyler once again seemed to come up with exactly what I needed to hear, giving me the insight I needed to finish the "variations" assignment *and* work the way I was comfortable.

"Do what you do best – copy the picture you've already got, then add something to it," he said.

"I'm not good at adding what's not there – that's my problem," I whispered back.

"So add something from another picture. You said your mom thinks the baby's going to be a perfect little angel, right? So paint her that way. Look at someone else's angel picture, and add whatever you need."

And in the end, that's exactly what I did.

I thought about how I'd viewed the baby at first, as an unwelcome intruder, and I drew her with a beret, and a black mask over her eyes – like a cat burglar creeping into my life.

Then I sketched her the way Mike and my mom saw her: as an angel, with wings, and a halo, and a heavenly glow all around her.

But even while I worked, I couldn't totally keep what had happened with Tyler off my mind. I found myself thinking again about the person I used to be, and who I was becoming. And when I was finished, even though it was supposed to be variations on the new baby, I realized that it was really just variations on me.

Conner called his project *Variations on The Happy Couple*. He'd started with a drawing of a good-looking man and woman, arms entwined, gazing happily into each other's eyes.

"That's how they see each other, when they're in love," Conner explained. "They overlook each other's flaws, and they don't notice each other's imperfections. Which is how it should be, if it's unconditional love."

Then he'd drawn the same people, but exaggerated some of their features, and added other, less flattering details, so they were a bit more paunchy around the middle, and his ears were bigger, and her nose was more pointed, and they both had acne.

"That's how other people might see them," Conner explained.

For the third drawing, he handed in a black sheet of paper.

"Because sometimes love is totally blind," he explained, "... and some people can't see their lovers for who they really are, any more than they can see who they've turned into themselves."

Mrs. Van der Straeten loved it.

Chapter 23

$\mathcal{I}$ realized in early November how right Mrs. Van Der Straeten was about the fact that there are many different ways to look at things, and that Conner was also right about the fact that people are sometimes blind to what's right in front of them.

My parents were still keeping close tabs on me, but they were trying to encourage me to redevelop my pre-Tyler interests, so when I said I was going to Ashley's one night, they saw it as an encouraging sign that I was moving on.

I saw it as a chance to finally be out with Tyler again, without them knowing.

Ashley was having a big party to celebrate the end of football season, and I was really looking forward to it, because Tyler and I had been sneaking around for weeks, but we hadn't been out together in public for a long time.

Tyler looked amazing, and he said I did too. We had trouble keeping our hands off each other, and everything seemed perfect.

A couple of hours into the party, someone suggested playing "Truth or Dare." Ashley passed around pieces of paper.

"Everyone write down a 'Truth' for someone to answer, or a 'Dare' for someone to do," she said. "And let's make it interesting, okay? We're not little kids anymore."

I couldn't think of anything to write, so I put, *"Who is the one person in this room, besides your date, that you would most like to make out with?"*

When all the papers had been collected, we sat in a circle, and one by one we drew the papers, and completed the "Truth" or "Dare."

One girl got *"Dare: kiss three people you just met."* She giggled the whole time, but she just pecked each one on the cheek.

Ashley got dared to take off an item of underwear in full view of everyone, but she unhooked her bra under her shirt and slid it out one of her sleeves, so it wasn't nearly as racy as everyone thought it would be.

The game went on like that, with a lot of laughter, but nothing too risqué happening, so I wasn't worried when it was my turn.

I got *"Dare: show everyone a part of your body that can get you into a lot of trouble. Hands don't count."*

I hooked one hand down over the top of my jeans, and then I wriggled my hips a little bit, as if I were going to pull them down – and I showed everyone my belly ring.

"This little thing got me into a *lot* of trouble," I said, circling the room to show everyone. "First *it* nearly killed me with blood poisoning, then *my parents* nearly killed me when they found out," I explained.

"Isn't it killing you that it got you grounded from seeing me?" Tyler asked.

"Oh yeah – that too," I laughed, still circling.

"I think we've seen enough, Caitlyn," he said, in a voice that told me he was upset about something. "It's my turn now." He drew a piece of paper, and read it out loud to the crowd.

"'Truth,'" he read. *"'Are you still a virgin?'"* He looked at the group, then turned back to me. I hoped my eyes told him to please, please not share such private information with everyone else.

"Nope," he said, with a devilish grin. Then he added, "And when I accidentally started dating one, I made sure she didn't stay that way either." Everyone laughed, and he reached out and patted me on the head like a puppy. A couple of the girls started whispering to each other, and Ashley looked at me with the shocked expression of someone who's just realized they don't really know anything about you. I was probably looking at Tyler the same way.

My face was hot with embarrassment, and knots had formed in my stomach. I pulled him out of the circle into a corner of the room, as the tears started rolling down my cheeks.

"How could you?" I hissed.

He shrugged. "Relax. It's the truth, so what's the problem?"

"It's the truth that you wouldn't be with me if we didn't have sex?"

He softened. "You know I love you, right?" he asked. "And we have sex because we love each other – so that was true."

"You didn't have to tell everyone like that, or make it sound so cheap and gross!" I sobbed.

"*Everyone* does it. Brandon's probably the only guy in this room who isn't getting any, so you don't need to be so touchy about it," he said. "And I'm tired of sneaking around all the time. I want everyone to know we love each other. Besides, I was trying to be funny, and you were a hard act to follow, after that striptease you did."

"I did *not* do a striptease!"

"Seemed like you wanted to – you were working every guy in the room but me," he said. Hurt and jealousy flashed in his eyes.

"So that's it?" I couldn't remember ever being so angry. "You're jealous of the belly ring *you* encouraged me to get? The one *you* signed for? The one *you* said would be hot and sexy? So then *you* can't stand if someone else sees it, so you mock our love, and humiliate me in front of my friends? *You're* an asshole!" I practically spat the words at him.

He slapped me – hard, right across the face, right in front of everyone. "Don't you ever speak to me like that again," he hissed.

In that instant, I saw him with a clarity I hadn't known in months. *Variations on the Theme of Tyler.* I saw him as he'd appeared to be at the beginning of our relationship – a handsome prince, ready to carry me off into the sunset. I saw him as I'd wanted him to be – a good man like Mike, fiercely loyal to the woman he loved. And I saw him as he really was – an insecure bully who couldn't love me without hurting and controlling me.

Ultimately, Conner would say that was the moment

when I stopped trying to make everything look perfect.

In learning to look at things abstractly, I'd finally seen them realistically. And I didn't like what I saw. I couldn't pretend the things Tyler did to me were accidents anymore.

Chapter 24

"Is it completely over?" Ashley asked me later that night, after Brandon had escorted Tyler out, and the other guests had gone.

"It has to be," I said.

"Because he hit you?" she asked.

"Yes and no," I told her, looking at the floor.

"What do you mean?" She sounded puzzled. "You can't keep seeing a guy who would hit you."

"I know that *now*. And I guess I knew it before ... but ..."

"But what?" she asked.

"The first time it happened, it seemed like an accident. I thought he loved me, so I tried to tell myself that everything would work out okay," I whispered, still not wanting to say it out loud. "But now everyone knows the truth."

Ashley took my hand, and I saw the concern in her face, so I went on.

"As long as it was just between him and me, I felt like it was my fault, like I was causing his bad moods, and I just had to work really hard to fix whatever was wrong – I could be a better girlfriend, love him more, make it right, and keep him happy. He's so great when he's happy – he really is," I explained, surprising myself a little with the answer. "And I know that was twisted, because it *was* wrong of him, even if nobody else was aware of it," I continued. "But somehow, when he humiliated me, and slapped me like that, and I knew I was going to have to come up with an explanation – not just for myself, but for everyone else in the room – I realized there *is* no explanation. Except that he's been treating me badly, and I haven't stood up for myself."

"You know," Ashley said gently, "you shouldn't have had to stand up for yourself. *He* should have treated you better."

I nodded, because I knew I'd start crying again if I said anything out loud.

"Anyway," she continued, "I'm glad it's over. We didn't like what was happening."

"You knew?" I asked.

"For a long time," she said. "Well – not the specific details, obviously, just that you were getting to be really unsure of yourself, and he seemed so controlling ... we kind of put two and two together."

"Who's 'we'?" I asked.

"All of us – me, Brandon, Conner. Everyone who cares about you."

"*Everyone?*" I couldn't believe what she was telling me. As hard as I had tried to keep it a secret, everyone had known anyway. I remembered what Dr. Mills had told me the day she'd treated me for the infection: "*Sometimes even when you take all the precautions, things can go wrong.*"

I changed Goldie's water that night when I got home.

"What are you doing?" my mom asked when she heard the water running. "It's almost midnight!"

"He needs a fresh start," I said. "We both do."

I saw the concern on her face, but I wasn't ready to say anything else to her yet.

The next day, I told my mother everything. I started

out just wanting to confess that Tyler and I had been in contact, but were done for good. I hadn't planned to tell her about the hitting, and the sleeping together, but then it all just sort of came out. Deep down, I must have known that she'd understand. I cried a lot, and she did too.

"I feel so awful for not realizing that you were in trouble," she said, as she held me.

"I don't think I understood myself how all of it was affecting me – so how could *you*?" I said.

"I might not have recognized all of it, but there *were* signs, now that I think about it," she said, with a shake of her head. "You were doing poorly in school, you weren't spending as much time with your friends ... Mike and I talked about it, but we really just thought it was a bit of sulking over the new baby. I'm so sorry I wasn't there for you."

I didn't tell Mike all the stuff that had happened, but I'm pretty sure my mom did, because he hugged me extra hard that night after dinner, and told me he couldn't believe how fast I'd grown up. I was kind of embarrassed, thinking that he might know about everything, but the fact that he didn't try to make me talk about it made things easier.

On Monday, my mom stayed home from work to take me to a counselor at a women's shelter.

"Aren't shelters for women who get beat up by their husbands?" I asked.

"They are, but they're also for girls who get hurt by their boyfriends," my mom said. "And I want you to talk to someone who really understands."

The counselor was nice. She said my mom had phoned her with a very brief explanation of my situation, but she asked me to go over everything with her in detail.

It was still hard to talk about, and I cried a lot more than I had even with my mom.

When I was done, she explained that because of the hitting, the force he'd used when I lost my virginity, and the way he tried to control who I saw and what I did, I had been the victim of physical, sexual, and emotional abuse.

"Tyler did slap me a couple of times," I said, "and I don't believe anymore that those were accidents, but it wasn't really *abuse* ... it's not like he punched me, or kicked me, or anything ..."

"Even if it only happens once, it's abuse," she said. "And it's not acceptable."

"Still, it wasn't all his fault," I started to say, still thinking I'd caused some of it, and wanting to protect him out of some old loyalty.

"Denial is one of the reasons people don't leave abusive relationships," she said softly. "Nobody wants to believe that someone they love would hurt them, so we make excuses, change our own behavior, and deny what's really happening."

I nodded, knowing she was right.

"My stepfather wants to call the police and have Tyler arrested or something," I confessed. "But I don't want him to ..."

"That's a decision you have to make for yourself," she said. "You *might* feel better if you get a restraining order, but then again, if you and your parents feel you're safe now, it might cause you more stress to get into the legalities of it all."

"Is it wrong that I kind of miss him already?" I asked.

"No, Caitlyn, it's not wrong. It's normal. My guess is that you wouldn't have stayed with him if he didn't have some wonderful qualities too."

"He did," I said.

She also talked to me about making a doctor's appointment.

"I understand that you've been through a rough time, Caitlyn, but there are health issues associated with being sexually active, and you need to talk to a doctor about it," she explained.

"I don't plan on having sex again anytime soon," I told her.

"That's okay. But when you *are* ready, it should be a positive experience for you, without the worry of unplanned pregnancies or STDs," she explained.

Together, we set up a series of appointments to talk again. Before I left, she said something really important: she told me it wasn't my fault.

Chapter 25

By the end of November, I was finally wrapping up my independent study project for art.

Mrs. Van der Straeten had given us some "*To think about ...*" questions for the closing statements on our artist's biography project. She wanted us to answer them, and append the responses to our written work.

I thought long and hard about my answer for "*How might learning about this artist influence your own work now, or in the future?*"

I wrote: "Learning about the art and life of Camille Claudel taught me that you have to take care of yourself first, because if you live in the darkness of someone else's shadow, you cannot grow healthy and strong, and your spirit will wither and die. Great art is full of spirit."

Looking at my self-portrait, I knew that's what it lacked: there was no spirit in the carefully controlled brushstrokes, and there was no spirit in my eyes, because for months there hadn't been any spirit in me.

"How do I fix this?" I asked Goldie. He stared back at me with his wet, fishy face, and somehow, he seemed to send me the answer.

Tyler had broken my spirit, but he hadn't killed it. I grabbed a brush and started painting.

I worked all week on the portrait. On the day it was due, the paint was still wet, but I was ready to present it to the class.

The background was black now, like the night I felt I'd just come through; but Goldie the Second shone like a beacon, representing the good that Tyler had brought me, and guiding me out of the darkness. A crown tilted on the side of my head, for the princess that I longed to be. There was blood spewing out from my belly ring – as if my insides had been destroyed, and they were being drained out of me against my will. I painted my heart as a thing that had just been ripped from my body, leaving a fresh wound behind. The heart itself wasn't completely broken, but was crisscrossed with scar tissue. Instead of bruises, I put footsteps on my body. Tears streamed from my eyes, but the mouth was firm and set in a defiant expression. Finally, I gave myself muscles – big, bulging, guy-type muscles – to remind myself that I am strong.

Talking about the painting was easier than I'd expected it to be. I began by describing the different features of the work, and I explained what each one of them represented.

It didn't *look* realistic – not in the way I usually painted. But it felt more realistic than anything else I'd done all year.

After the showing, I read the comments submitted by my classmates in their peer evaluations.

Cool. Looks like a chick you don't want to mess with.

Sometimes I feel like that – like my insides are spilling out, and everyone can see my private thoughts.

You tried to paint the ugly truth, but you're still beautiful, inside and out.

I just knew that Conner had written the last one.

I continued to see my counselor, and Tyler continued to try to contact me by phone and email, and occasionally by showing up in person. Refusing to talk to him was hard, because I really missed his sweet side. But I knew I couldn't change him, so I had to change myself.

With Tyler mostly out of my life, and my mom getting bigger and bigger, I found myself spending more time with Mike. We shopped, and cooked, and even watched television together while Mom rested.

One night, Mike asked for my help to surprise her.

"Caitlyn, I've been thinking about the baby's room. The wall color is fine, but I'd really like to make it something special for her, and for your mother. Would you paint a mural in there? For your little sister?"

"A mural? You mean, something that takes up a whole wall?"

"Exactly."

"What kind of picture are you thinking about?"

"I think you should decide that," he said. "You have such a gift – pick something wonderful that you'd like to share with the baby, and put it up on the wall for her to enjoy every day."

"But I don't know what I should paint ..." I said.

"Give it time. Something will come to you," he reassured me. "And, Caitlyn? The baby is going to be lucky to have you for her sister."

"She's going to be lucky to have you for a dad," I told him. Then I added, "We both are."

The holidays came and went, and winter settled in. I worked hard on the mural, but I wouldn't let anyone in to see it. I told them that since it was going to be the baby's room, she should be the first one to look at it. My mom spent most of February on bed rest, and went into hospital for the last week of her pregnancy. Finally, in March, she had her first labor pains.

My little sister was tiny, and wrinkly, and red, and yet somehow she was still the most beautiful little person I'd ever seen.

"She doesn't look like an 'Elizabeth' after all," my mom said, trying out the name she'd chosen months ago. "What do you think, Caitlyn?"

"I think she's a perfect little angel," I said. "And I mean that in a good way."

We named her Angelique.

When she came home, I picked her up gently and took her to her nursery.

"This used to be my room," I explained, "but now it's yours. I've painted it just like your very own ice cream parlor," I told her, carrying her past the rainbow colored walls. "I know you haven't tried ice cream yet, but when you do, you're going to find out that, even though it almost always tastes good, some kinds are better than others. Don't get stuck on any one flavor right away – try a few, until you find the best."

She drooled a bit, and I imagined that some part of her actually understood what I was trying to tell her.

"Over here is our family," I said, pointing to the people at the counter. "It was mine first, like the room, but now I'm sharing it with you. It's our family. It's one of the most important things I have, and I almost forgot that this year. I put it in here to remind you, so you don't make the same mistakes I did. That's Mom, and this is our dad. You're over here between them. See? We might have to change your picture a little bit, because you're going to grow, and get bigger. And that's me – that one's going to keep changing too."

Tyler called me the next day. He'd seen the birth announcement in the local paper.

"Congratulations on your new sister," he said.

"Thanks."

"Is she a monstrous test-tube mutant?" he asked, "Or is she really cute, like you?" I could hear the old charm in his voice.

"She's pretty awesome," I told him.

"How's Goldie the Second?" he asked.

"You know I'll always love him," I said, hoping he didn't hear my voice catch.

"I hope he knows how lucky he is," he said softly. He paused for a minute, then continued. "Hey ... umm ... I was wondering – about that big painting you did? You know, the self-portrait? How did it turn out?" he asked.

I looked at my self-portrait across the room, and I thought about how much it had already changed.

Now, every time I resist Tyler's pleas for forgiveness, I pierce the blackness of the portrait's background with a gold star for myself. The stars remind me of my strength. Though I don't yet have enough stars to obliterate the darkness, someday I will.

"It's a work in progress," I said.

The End

Fighting the Current
by Heather Waldorf
Hardcover ISBN: 978-1-894222-93-8
Paperback ISBN: 978-1-894222-92-1

Theresa "Tee" Stanford figures her life is smooth sailing. But everything changes when a drunk driver hits her father, leaving him mentally disabled. With her last year of high school looming large and a friendship teetering on the brink of romance, Tee finds she can no longer rely on her old plans for the future.

"The characters are believably imperfect, and they work through their troubles in realistic ways." – *School Library Journal*

"You are drawn in ... from the very first page ... This is a very intense, very real book." – *Independently Reviewed*

"A meaty read, *Fighting the Current* will leave thoughtful readers ... asking 'Who am I?' " – *CM: Canadian Review of Materials*

Selected, International Reading Association Young Adults' Choices (2006)

Shortlisted, Stellar Book Award (BC Teen Readers' Choice Awards, 2006-2007)

Winner, USA Book News "Best Books Awards", Young Adult Fiction Category (2005)

Selected, Children's Book Committee at Bank Street College, Teen Booklist

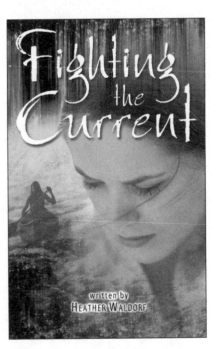

www.lobsterpress.com